PENGUIN BOOKS

THE TAROT

Alfred Douglas was born in England in 1942. Inspired
by his family's interest in arcane tradition, he began
to study occult symbolism when he was still very
young. His attraction to Oriental beliefs and practices
led to his first full-length work, *How to Consult the
I Ching*, published in 1971. He is a member of the
College of Psychic Studies and of the celebrated
Society for Psychical Research, the oldest organiza-
tion of its kind in the world. A regular contributor
to the journal *Prediction* and a frequent guest on
British radio and television, Douglas divides his time
between an apartment in London and a house in
Whitby, where Bram Stoker wrote *Dracula*, on the
rugged coast of the Yorkshire moors.

Alfred Douglas

THE TAROT

The Origins, Meaning and Uses of the Cards

Illustrated by David Sheridan

Penguin Books

Penguin Books Ltd, Harmondsworth, Middlesex, England
Penguin Books Inc, 7110 Ambassador Road,
Baltimore, Maryland 21207, U.S.A.
Penguin Books Australia Ltd, Ringwood, Victoria, Australia

First published in the United States by
Taplinger Publishing Co., Inc., New York, 1972
First published in Great Britain by Victor Gollancz Ltd, London, 1973
Published by Penguin Books Inc, 1973
Published by Penguin Books Ltd, 1974

Copyright © Alfred Douglas, 1972
Original drawings copyright © David Sheridan, 1972

Printed in the United States of America

FRONTISPIECE:
The twenty-two cards of the Tarot major trumps
arranged in a figure-of-eight
(Drawings by David Sheridan)

To
my old friend
MADELINE MONTALBAN
who introduced me to
the Tarot

Acknowledgements

Grateful acknowledgement is herewith made to the following publishers for their kind permission to quote from titles published by them:

To George Allen & Unwin Ltd., publishers of *Schopenhauer's Essays* translated by Thomas Bailey Saunders.

To Rider and Company, publishers of *Transcendental Magic* and *A History of Magic* by Eliphas Lévi, and *The Tarot of the Bohemians* by Papus.

To Routledge & Kegan Paul Ltd. and to Princeton University Press, publishers of *The Structure and Dynamics of the Psyche* and *Psychology and Alchemy*, volumes 8 and 12 of the collected works of C. G. Jung, edited by G. Adler, M. Fordham, H. Read, translated by R. F. C. Hull (Bollingen series XX); and *Aurora Consurgens*, edited by Marie-Louise von Franz, translated by R. F. C. Hull and A. S. B. Glover (Bollingen series LXXVII).

Thanks are also due to the Trustees of the British Museum for their courtesy in allowing the reproduction of items in their collection of playing cards.

The author would also like to record his appreciation of the help extended to him during his researches by Professor Mario Tassoni and Miss Liana Borghi of the Italian Institute, London; and to Mr Adriano Lombardini of Bergamo, Italy, for permission to reproduce cards from the Masenghini Tarocco pack.

The Tarot designs reproduced on pages 28–29 were photographed by John Freeman; all the other photographs are the work of Barry Rolfe.

Contents

Preface

WHAT ARE TAROT CARDS?

TAROT CARDS ARE probably the original European playing cards, the forerunners of our modern pack; but the standard Tarot pack differs from its more familiar descendent in several ways.

For example, it is made up of a total of seventy-eight cards instead of only fifty-two. Also, it is really two packs combined—a fifty-six card pack called the *lesser arcana* or *small cards*, and a twenty-two card pack called the *greater arcana* or *Tarot trumps*.

The lesser arcana of the Tarot is the source of present-day playing cards. The fifty-six cards are divided into four suits called, in Italian, *Bastoni* (Batons or Clubs), *Coppes* (Cups), *Spade* (Swords), and *Denari* (Coins). Each suit is made up of ten cards numbered from Ace (1) to 10, with the addition of four court cards called the *Re* (King), *Dama* (Queen), *Cavallo* (Knight) and *Fante* (Knave or Jack).

English and American playing cards of today show French suit-marks which first came into use in the early 15th century. These are called *Trèfles* (Trefoils), *Coeurs* (Hearts), *Piques* (Pikes), and *Carreaux* (Paving Tiles); equivalent to the English Clubs, Hearts, Spades and Diamonds. Curiously enough, the names of three of the English suits are derived from the Italian Tarot: Spades from the Italian Spade, Clubs from Bastoni, and Diamonds from Denari. Only the suit of Hearts takes its name from the French cards.

The remaining part of the Tarot, the twenty-two card greater arcana, is now only used in certain parts of the world. Only one of its cards has affected the transition to the fifty-two card pack. The trump card entitled The Fool has survived as the Joker.

Each card of the greater arcana depicts a symbolical figure or scene and has a descriptive title printed at the bottom of it. The

cards are numbered, in Roman numerals, from I to XXI, only
The Fool having no number assigned to it.

Prior to about 1750 all Tarot trumps seem to have been named
in Italian, but most later packs give the titles in French. The word
"Tarot" comes from the French cards. In Italy they are called
Tarocchi. The origin and meaning of this word is not known.

Here are the titles of the twenty-two major trump cards in
Italian, French and English, given in their usual order:

	Il Matto	Le Fou (or Le Mat)	The Fool
I	Il Bagattel	Le Bateleur	The Magician
II	La Papessa	La Papesse	The Female Pope
III	L'Imperatrice	L'Impératrice	The Empress
IV	L'Imperator	L'Empereur	The Emperor
V	Il Papa	Le Pape	The Pope
VI	Gli Amanti	L'Amoureux	The Lover(s)
VII	Il Carro	Le Chariot	The Chariot
VIII	La Giustizia	La Justice	Justice
IX	L'Eremita	L'Ermite (or Le Capuchin)	The Hermit
X	Ruota della Fortuna	Roue de Fortune	Wheel of Fortune
XI	La Forza	La Force	Fortitude
XII	L'Apesso (or Lo Impichato)	Le Pendu	The Hanged Man
XIII	La Morte (or unnamed)	(Unnamed)	Death
XIV	La Temperanza	Temperance	Temperance
XV	Il Diavolo	Le Diable	The Devil
XVI	La Torre	La Maison de Dieu	The Tower
XVII	Le Stelle	L'Etoile	The Star
XVIII	La Luna	La Lune	The Moon
XIX	Il Sole	Le Soleil	The Sun
XX	Il Gindizio (or L'Angelo)	Le Jugement	Judgement
XXI	Il Mondo	Le Monde	The World

Despite the popularity of the less complicated fifty-two card
pack, Tarot cards have retained a loyal following in some parts of
Europe, and they are still being manufactured today. You
will find the full seventy-eight card Tarot in use in Italy,
Czechoslovakia, France, Switzerland, Yugoslavia and parts of
North Africa.

Also, as a result of the current resurgence of interest in divination and other aspects of the occult, Tarot cards can be found on sale in major cities in practically every country in the West.

Although the cards were established in Italy, France and Germany by the late 14th century, the time, place and circumstances of their creation remains a mystery. The complex and beautiful designs of the twenty-two greater arcana cards in particular provide an enigma that has never been satisfactorily resolved. Who made them and what are they meant to illustrate? Nobody knows for certain.

THE TAROT

1

THE ORIGIN OF TAROT CARDS

IT IS GENERALLY accepted by scholars that the earliest playing cards originated in China and Korea, where examples have been found dating back to at least the 11th century. The design of these cards appears to have been based on paper money, which evolved during the T'ang dynasty (618–908).

One must regretfully reject the solution offered by the Chinese dictionary *Ching-tze-tung* of 1678 which claims that playing cards were invented in 1120 for the amusement of the Emperor's concubines.

Early packs of cards from Southern China frequently have four suits, called Coins, Strings of Coins, Myriads of Strings, and Tens of Myriads. It is feasible that such packs provided inspiration for the first makers of European cards, having been brought back by merchants returning from the East. But there is no evidence to support this theory—although the idea of using paper money was brought West from China at this time.

Western playing cards do not resemble their Eastern counterparts closely, either in shape or design.

One old theory suggests that cards originated in India. The four-armed Hindu diety Ardhanari, an androgynous figure combining the right half of the god Siva with the left half of his consort Devi, is sometimes depicted holding a cup, a sceptre, a sword and a ring. The monkey-god Hanuman is also at times shown holding these same emblems, which bear a close resemblance to the four suit-signs of the Tarot pack: Cups, Batons, Swords and Coins.

Unfortunately there is no evidence to reveal how old these symbols are or whether they ever appeared on Indian playing cards, which are generally circular and bear little resemblance to European cards.[1]

Western playing cards first appeared in India during the 16th century, having been carried there by travellers from Europe. We must discount, alas, the legend that playing cards were invented by the wife of a Maharajah, to distract him from his infuriating habit of pulling his beard.

According to the Italian author Covelluzo, writing in 1480, cards were introduced into Italy in 1379 from North Africa. Covelluzo says: *"Anno 1379, fu recato in Viterbo el gioco delle carte, che venne de Seracinia, e chiamisi tra loro naib"* ("In the year 1379 the game of cards was brought into Viterbo from the country of the Saracens, where it is called naib.")[2]

The Arabs might have brought playing cards with them to Europe. After expanding across Africa and Asia they had first attempted to cross the Mediterranean in the 7th century. They entered Spain around 710, penetrated France as far as Arles by 731, had conquered Sicily by 832 and set foot on the Italian mainland around 842. Later, they were hired as mercenaries by the Popes and feuding Italian princes.

In 1379 they formed part of the paid armies of the rival Popes Urban VI and Clement VII. According to Covelluzo the Saracens called the game of cards *naib*; significantly, cards in Spain are called *naipes*, and the Arabs also occupied Southern Spain until 1492.

However, *naipes* may be derived from the Flemish word *knaep*, meaning paper, as a lively sea-trade existed between Spain and Flanders at this time. Another fact counting against Covelluzo's theory is that there is no mention of playing cards in the Arabian Nights, which would surely have described them if they had been in common use among the Arabs.

Also, records attest that by 1379 cards were known in France, Switzerland and as far north as Belgium.

One widespread belief, still popular today, is that the pack was brought into Europe by fortune-telling Gypsies coming from either Egypt or India. But the Gypsies did not appear in the West in any numbers until the middle of the 15th century, a full hundred years after the cards were known in every country from Italy to Northern France. The Gypsies adopted them and did much to spread them abroad, but they did not invent playing cards.[3]

The invention of Tarot cards has also been attributed to the Order of the Knights Templar, an ascetic military Order founded c. 1188 by Hugh de Payens and eight fellow knights to protect pilgrims and guard the routes to the Holy Land.

The Templars gained Papal approval and were awarded privileges such as immunity from taxes and secular jurisdiction. Over the years they attained a position of great wealth and power and thus made many enemies. Finally, at the beginning of the 14th century, Philip IV of France brought the charge of heresy against the Order. In 1307 Templars in France were arrested and their property seized; many were tortured by the Inquisition into confessing heretical beliefs. The persecution quickly spread to all other countries where the Templars had property, and the Order was finally eradicated in 1314 when its Grand Master, Jacques de Molay, was burned at the stake whilst declaring his innocence.[4]

The charges laid against the Templars were both contradictory and unproven. Their long years in the East may have laid them open to Gnostic influences, but this has not been established. There is no evidence to connect them with the Tarot cards, or to suggest parallels between their beliefs and the Tarot images.

All the evidence suggests that although the idea of playing cards may have been brought to the West from elsewhere, the designs we are familiar with originated inside Europe. The question is— where?

Many commentators have tried to find a clue hidden in the meaning of the word "Tarot". Some have asserted that it is derived from an ancient Egyptian word, *Ta-rosh*, meaning "The royal way". Others have asserted that it is an anagram of the Latin word *rota*, meaning "a wheel"—the cards then symbolising the circle of life from birth to death.

Still others have derived it from *Torah*, Hebrew for "the law", hoping to link the cards with the mystical system of the Qabalah but forgetting that the Qabalah originated in Spain, a country which has never known the Tarot major trumps.

Some have seen in it a corruption of the name *Thoth*, the ancient Egyptian god of magic, so reaffirming the legend that the cards were created in the initiation temples of the mysterious East.

Tarot is the name given to the cards in France. In Italy they are called "Tarocco" (plural Tarocchi,) and in other countries Taro, Taroc, or Tarok. It is not known which of these, if any, is the original form.

If the four suits of the pack were derived from the cards of China, then the court cards (said to be originally *coat* cards as they depicted richly garbed figures) may have been taken from figures used in the game of chess, which had reached Europe via India and the Holy Land at the time of the First Crusade (1095–9).

The twenty-two allegorical trump cards may not have formed part of the original pack. The earliest undisputed reference to playing cards which we have, a detailed description of cards and card games made by a German monk living in a Swiss monastery in 1377, makes no mention of these striking designs.[5]

However, the major trumps were certainly in existence in 1415, when a beautiful hand-painted Tarot pack was created for the young Duke of Milan, Filippo Maria Visconti.[6]

Cards are not mentioned in the works of Boccaccio (1313–75) or Petrarch (1304–74), but the majority of the most celebrated later packs were hand-painted for members of the great families of Northern Italy, such as the Visconti, Este, and Sforza. It is also a fact that until around 1750 all Tarot packs had Italian suit-marks. After this date packs produced outside Italy generally had French suits and different major trump designs.

It used to be believed that the oldest cards still in existence were French. Seventeen of these cards—sixteen of them major trumps of the Tarot—are in the Bibliothèque Nationale at Paris.[7]

It was long thought that these beautiful hand-painted cards formed part of the pack made in 1392 for Charles VI of France and recorded in his treasurer's book of accounts for February of that year. But there is no connection between this passage and the seventeen cards in the Bibliothèque Nationale, and the artistic style and details of dress shown in the cards places them later in time than 1392.

If Tarot cards—as seems most likely—were devised originally somewhere in Northern Italy it can be surmised that their makers were perhaps inspired by oriental cards brought from the East by merchants returning to the great trading port of Venice. The original seventy-eight card Tarot pack is generally referred to in

Italy as the Venetian or Piedmontese Pack to differentiate it from later offshoots such as the ninety-seven card Florentine minchiate pack and the sixty-two card Bolognese pack.

It is even possible that the cards were named after their place of origin. The North Italian plain is watered by the river Po, an important tributary of which is the river Taro.

Most of the historical evidence we have regarding the first appearance of playing cards in Europe is of a negative kind. Reference to town records can tell us when they became widespread enough to be worthy of note or condemnation, but not how long it took for them to become popular or where they came from.

Here is a summary of the known references to cards in the 14th century and later. Some earlier mentions are claimed, but these are all disputed.

1275	Games are mentioned in the Townbook of Augsburg, Germany, but cards are not referred to.
1289–99	The Code of Nuremberg, Germany, does not include cards amongst its list of prohibited games.
1328–41	A French manuscript, "Renard le Contrefait", written between these dates, contains a passage that might refer to cards.
1377	Cards and card games are described by a monk at the monastery of Brefeld, Switzerland.
1378	Cards are banned in Regensburg, Germany.
1379	The purchase of cards is recorded in the accounts of the Dukedom of Brabant (Belgium).
1380–84	Cards are permitted by the Code of Nuremberg.
1381	Cards are condemned in the records of a notary of Marseilles, France.
1392	The treasurer's accounts of Charles VI of France includes a payment for three packs of handmade cards.
1393	Cards are listed amongst the permitted games in Florence.
1397	A decree in Paris includes cards amongst a list of games forbidden to commoners on working days.
1415	Tarot cards are painted for the Duke of Milan.
1423	Cards are condemned in a speech made at Bologna by

St Bernardin of Siena. He does not refer to the Tarot major trumps.

1423–77	Townbooks of Nuremberg name several women as card-painters.
1427	Two Master Card-makers are named in the Guild registers of Brabant.
1440	The earliest surviving cards printed from wood-blocks —they are French court cards.
1440	Playing cards are printed at Stuttgart.
1441	The importation of foreign playing cards is prohibited by the authorities of Venice.
1450–70	A Franciscan Friar preaches a sermon in Northern Italy condemning dice and cards. He makes a clear distinction between the four suits and the twenty-two major trumps.
1463	The importation of foreign cards into England is forbidden in a statute of Edward IV, to protect home manufacturers.

It can be seen from the above table that the invention of wood-block printing in Germany in the early 15th century heralded the start of a large-scale card manufacturing industry. The fact that cards were banned in Regensburg as early as 1378 implies that cheap stencilled packs were being produced in quantities at an earlier date, as ordinary people could not possibly afford to purchase the sort of hand-painted packs which were supplied to the nobility.

Popular demand for cards far outweighed religious opposition to them, and by the mid-15th century card-making workshops were thriving in many cities of Italy, France, Germany and Belgium. Considering the variety of new games and new cards to play them with which developed from this time onwards, it is remarkable that the early designs survived at all.

There is a strong possibility that the twenty-two Tarot trumps evolved independently of the four suits. They are not mentioned by Brother Johannes of Brefeld in 1377, and although the existence of the Visconti Tarot in 1415 proves that they were known at that time, the speech made by the Franciscan Friar in Northern Italy somewhere between 1450 and 1470 clearly differentiates between them and the remaining cards.

If this is so, the time and circumstances in which the two packs were combined remains a mystery.

The Tarot pack has undergone many alterations during its lifetime. The version which has deviated least from the early Venetian Tarocco is probably the French *Tarot de Marseilles*, which is based on quite early woodblock prints.

All modern Italian packs are made up of double-headed cards which are more convenient for card games. But as each of the major trumps and court cards has had the lower half of its design removed and the top half repeated in an inverted position beneath, much of the symbolism is destroyed. In the trump card called The Hanged Man, for example, one is presented with a meaningless picture of two lower torsos joined at the waist.

But considering the changes that have taken place in playing card design over the centuries, it is remarkable that these complex and enigmatic designs have retained so much of their original character during six hundred years of continuous production.

2

THE SYMBOLISM OF THE TAROT

As well as the question of where and when Tarot cards first appeared, there is also the puzzle of their original meaning and purpose. Perhaps by examining the civilisation which produced them we may arrive at some helpful conclusions.

The Medieval Renaissance

A great revival of learning took place in Western Europe during the 11th, 12th and 13th centuries. It was an age of great energy and curiosity, when men were becoming aware of new possibilities inherent in the world around them.

Europe was then an open society in many ways, in which new ideas and beliefs came together and intermingled in great profusion. These were drawn partly from the classical past which was now being rediscovered, and partly from other areas of the world with which communication was being established along the newly-opened trade-routes.[1]

From the mid-11th century the routes to the Near and Far East, and the Eastern Mediterranean, were dominated by the maritime cities of Northern Italy. Their merchants benefited from the decline of Byzantium as a great trading power, and later, in the 12th and early 13th centuries, the cities of Venice, Genoa and Pisa consolidated their position even further when they acted as transporters and suppliers to the crusaders heading East.

The Italian traders established good relations with the Islamic merchants with whom they dealt in the Near East, and also with rulers in more distant places. Nicolo and Maffeo Polo, for example, first traded with Kublai Khan at Peking in 1266, and when they took Nicolo's son Marco to China with them in 1271 he remained there in the service of the Mongol Empire for fifteen years, only returning home in 1291.

The Mongol society was tolerant of all religions which did not threaten it, and the Italians found themselves in the company of Buddhists, Confucianists, Taoists, Shamanists, Moslems, Jews, Nestorian Christians and members of Gnostic and other sects.

The merchants of inland Italian cities, particularly those of Lombardy, controlled the Savoy passes and therefore the trade-routes to the North. This enabled them to attend the great fairs of Champagne, and the important commercial and industrial centres of Flanders, France and the north-west of Germany. Such contacts led in turn to further trading opportunities with England, Scandinavia and Russia.

This was before the Church in the West began to fear any threat to its own position, and new ideas could be openly discussed without a charge of heresy being brought. The merchants of Italy were not only resourceful businessmen and daring travellers, they also had bright and enquiring minds which were stimulated by the new religions and cultures to which they were exposed.

As a result, alien philosophies spread rapidly through Northern Italy, into France and the Rhineland, and thence to other parts of the continent.

The North of Italy and the South of France were culturally very close at this time; many Italians went to live in Provence and from there opened up trading relations with Spain and the Moorish-dominated Western Mediterranean. Many of the cities of Italy, France and Spain in the 12th and 13th centuries were multi-racial, and Christians, Moslems and Jews existed amicably together.

One of the most important intellectual activities of this time was translation. Arabic, Jewish and other foreign works were made available to the scholars of Europe for the first time, and some cities, for example Toledo in Spain and Montpellier in France, were famous for the number and quality of the translations they produced.

The Norman conquest of England in the late 11th century had also opened the way for the dissemination of Celtic beliefs, leading to the popularisation of the "Matter of Britain", the Arthurian and Grail legends which entered the European mainstream through the courts of Northern France.

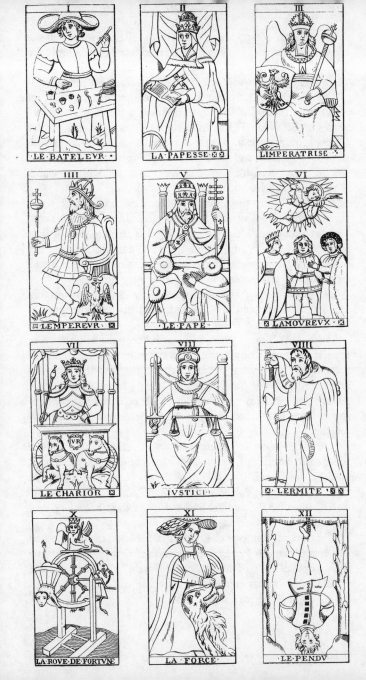

The twenty-two major trumps of the Tarot as depicted in a typical 18th-century pack. Although many errors in the spelling and punctuation of the titles of the cards can be seen, most details of the original images themselves have been faithfully reproduced.

So the medieval world presents us with a rich fabric of civilisation made up of material drawn from many sources. The art and literature of the 12th and 13th centuries reflected Western man's increasing concern for his interior development, and his awareness of a need for psychological growth and a greater degree of spiritual maturity than the hidebound teachings of the established church could offer or sustain.

Examples of such questioning can be seen in the works of early medieval scholars such as Bernard Sylvester,[2] who lived in the mid-12th century and who wrote several works including a commentary on the first books of the Aeneid, a verse translation of an Arabic work on astrological geomancy, and a long poem chronicling the outcome of an astrologer's prediction.

His most noted work, however, was a piece of philosophical speculation entitled *De Mundi Universitate* ("Concerning the universal nature of the world"), which he wrote between 1145 and 1153.

In this book Sylvester discusses the great Mother Goddess of antiquity (whom he calls *Natura*), Eros, the fecundating power of nature, and the nature of the stars, which he declares are gods.

Although this work is neo-Platonic and non-Christian in outlook, it was a great success in its time, and was still being studied and discussed in centres of learning such as Avignon, Pavia and Paris during the late middle ages.

Gnostic influences on Medieval thought

The trend towards a resurgence of interest in Pagan Classical

---

Twelve major trump cards from a French *Tarot de Marseilles* pack produced c.1900. Card II, The Papess, has here been replaced by *Junon*, and card V, The Pope, by *Jupiter*. The voicing of Papal disapproval in 1725 resulted in the deletion of four cards—The Papess, The Empress, The Emperor, and The Pope—from many packs, and the substitution of four Moors or Satraps in their place. Around 1800, in Besançon, The Papess and The Pope were replaced by Juno and Jupiter (as in the cards reproduced here), and during the revolution The Empress and The Emperor were replaced in Strasbourg by cards called The Grandfather (Le Grandprêtre) and The Grandmother (La Grandprêtresse). Modern French cards have reverted to the original designs. (British Museum: Willshire collection).

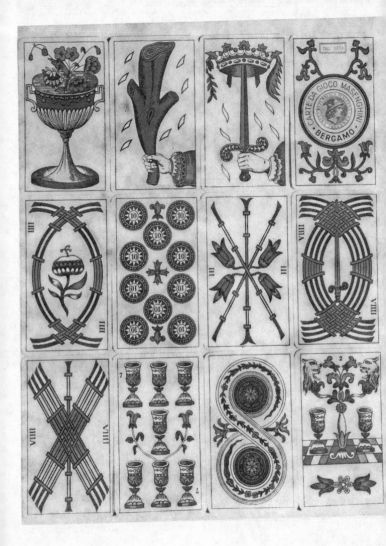

beliefs is best illustrated by the success of Gnostic religious sects in Europe at this time.[3]

The most striking example of this success is that of Catharism. The Cathars—their name was derived from a Greek word meaning "pure"—formed a dualistic sect which flourished mainly in the South of France and Northern Italy during the 12th and 13th centuries. They were also known as Albigenses after the name of one of their chief centres, the town of Albi, near Toulouse.[4]

The Cathars first made their presence felt in Languedoc around 1140, but their philosophy was probably carried there from Lombardy. A study of their doctrines reveals that they were descended from the Bogomils, a sect founded in Bulgaria around the year 940, reputedly by a priest called Bogomil.

This sect became very popular in the southern Balkans and in Asia Minor in the 10th and 11th centuries, and its main teachings seem to have been derived from the Paulisians, a Christian heretical sect which had arisen in Armenia and was probably an offshoot of the Manichean religion of Persia.[5]

Dualism is the name given to the belief that the universe is the battleground of two opposed powers. The world we know is thought of as being essentially evil, having been created by a malevolent power, the demiurge. This power was identified by Christian dualists with Satan.

The body and lower psyche of man was created by the demiurge, but contains within it an imprisoned spark of the opposing principle, the Godhead, which can only become free through a liberating enlightenment that will burst its material fetters. The

Twelve cards from a modern Italian Tarocco pack produced by Masenghini, Bergamo. These designs follow the earliest known patterns very closely: swords are depicted as curved, interlaced blades, batons are similar in appearance but straight, coins are elaborate medallions with the number of the card in the centre of each, and cups are tall and narrow and colourfully decorated. The masculine suits of batons and swords are numbered in Roman numerals, whilst the feminine suits of cups and coins are numbered in Arabic numerals. The ace of coins traditionally gives details of the manufacturer and of duty payable on the pack. The 2 of coins incorporates the figure-of-eight symbol which occurs frequently in the headdresses of the major trump and court card figures. (Author's collection.)

attainment of such self-knowledge was the declared aim of the dualists, who were called Gnostics after the Greek word *gnosis*, meaning "knowledge".

The Cathars of Europe believed not only that the physical world was the creation of the Devil, but that the Devil was in fact the God of the Old Testament.

They saw Christ as a saviour sent to reveal the way by which man could free himself from the bonds of matter, and to unmask the true nature of the Old Testament God. Totally rejecting the material world, they denied the Catholic Church's teachings regarding the physical resurrection of Christ and the bodily rebirth of the faithful on the Day of Judgement.

The Gnostic theme of the major trumps

It has been suggested that the Tarot cards might have been produced by Cathars as a means of representing their doctrines pictorially to those who were illiterate, but the Tarot images do not reflect Catharist beliefs in detail.

However, if the twenty-two cards of the greater arcana, the major trumps, are viewed in sequence—commencing with the unnumbered card The Fool and finishing with card XXI The World—they reveal the theme of Classical Gnosticism remarkably well:

Man's spirit is divine but is imprisoned in a physical body and is ignorant of its divinity (The Fool).

A messenger from higher spheres demonstrates his mastery of the material world and therefore proves the existence of something deeper than surface reality. In some accounts he becomes a teacher and companion to the fool (The Magician).

Before liberation can be aspired to, the ruling powers of the world (represented by The Papess, The Empress, The Emperor, and The Pope) must be withstood and the challenges of everyday existence met and surmounted (The Lovers and The Chariot).

Only when he has attained a degree of maturity can the seeker (The Hermit) commence the journey which will lead him back to his spiritual home.

His deliberate introversion (The Wheel of Fortune) demands the overcoming of physical urges (Fortitude) and the reversal of everyday values in a deliberate sacrifice of the lower to the higher (The Hanged Man).

The sublimation of the lower self (Death) leads to an influx of spiritual energy (Temperance) which enables him to defeat the demiurge (The Devil).

This leads to the shattering of his earthly prison (The Tower) and allows the passage of his spirit up through the Heavenly Spheres (The Star, The Sun and The Moon) until he can experience the mystical rebirth (Judgement) and finally merge with the *Anima Mundi*, the supra-personal Spirit of the World (The World).

To the Gnostic, the human spirit is a part of God, a "Divine Spark", and it suffers not for its own sins but as the result of a primeval tragedy over which it had no control.

Thus the redemption of man is also the redemption of God, and when the world is defeated it is a part of God which is released, enabling it to return to its source.

The symbolism of the Tarot cards can be seen to have more in common with the mystery religions of the Pagan classical world, as revealed in the teachings of Gnostics such as Basilides and Valentinus (2nd century A.D.) than with their Medieval descendants.[6]

This is not to say that such teachings did not survive into the 12th and 13th centuries. Manicheism, for example, a Gnostic religion founded in the 3rd century by a Persian Prince called Mani, spread throughout the East and remained one of the dominant religions of Asia for a thousand years.[7] The question of what other lesser-known bodies of tradition filtered West at this time remains open.

The varied sources of Tarot imagery

As we have seen, the origin of Tarot cards is not as easily traced as might at first be thought. They were created at a time when many streams of ideas were converging on Europe, and they are in all probability not the product of any one single tradition.

The designs were executed in Europe, but seem to incorporate not only Christian, Gnostic and Islamic imagery, but Celtic and Norse elements as well.

33

This can be seen just by looking at the cards:

The Hanged Man brings to mind the self-sacrifice of Odin on the World-tree, the symbolic death of Dionysus in the Orphic mysteries, and the initiatory tests carried out by Shamanists in the East.

The Lightning-struck Tower suggests parallels with the Bolt of Jove and its Norse equivalent the Hammer of Thor, and with the lightning-flash of enlightenment described in Mahayana and Tantric Buddhism, the flame in which all illusions are destroyed.

The High Priestess and The Empress are clear descendents of the goddesses of Wisdom and Fertility, Death and Life, of the ancient world, whilst The Star, The Moon and The Sun bring to mind Arabian and Classical astrology, the Astral Planes of the Gnostics, and the Divine Spheres of Dante.[8]

The Magician is Hermes Trismegistos, patron of alchemists and supreme god of the Gnosis who is also the trickster, the juggler who deceives by sleight-of-hand.

Card VI, The Lovers, is dominated by the pagan figure of Eros whilst card XX, Judgement, depicts an apocalyptic scene familiar to both Christians and Moslems.

The Art of Memory

There is no surviving record of Tarot cards being put to any use other than that of gaming and divination, yet it is known that other complex allegorical pictures were being produced in Medieval Europe as aids to memory and as a means of giving religious instruction to the illiterate.

Such designs would be carefully constructed from stock images which would suggest certain ideas or stories to the observer. In this way a complete Gospel, for example, could be represented symbolically in a way which might be "read" by anyone familiar with the conventions being used.

These techniques formed part of the "Art of Memory". Although memory treatises were not printed until about 1482 they are known to have circulated widely in manuscript form long before this date, being based on the revived learning of the Classical world.[9]

Some of the Tarot trumps can be fitted easily into their medieval framework: three of the Four Virtues—Justice, Temperance and Fortitude—are here, but where is Prudence? Perhaps it is symbolised by The Hermit, or even The Papess. Or maybe Prudence is allocated to the whole Tarot sequence; the Art of Memory was said to come under the auspices of Prudence.

The game of Triumphs

It has been recorded that the twenty-two major trumps of the Tarot were used in Renaissance Italy for playing a game called "Triumphs", which suggests another possible line of enquiry.

Festivals and processions formed a popular part of the fabric of urban life in Medieval and Renaissance Europe, nowhere more so than in Italy. Originally these were probably Mystery plays, dramatisations of sacred stories, but later they gave rise to ecclesiastical and secular processions given in honour of saints or visiting dignitaries.

Such splendid productions were often directed by famous artists—Brunelleschi and Leonardo da Vinci are two who are known to have designed mechanisms for animating elaborate tableaux—and were known as *Trionfi*, or "Triumphs".[10]

Whether the Tarot game of Triumphs was given its title because its originator thought that the cards were meant to depict a Triumphal procession, or whether the cards were indeed originally connected with some since-lost Mystery play, is, like so much of Tarot history, not known.

The minor cards of the Tarot pack

When we come to examine the cards of the lesser arcana the number of possible sources for its symbolism seems far less bewildering.

Here we have fifty-six cards divided into four suits, each suit containing four court cards and ten numbered cards.

The court cards depict Kings, Queens, Knights, and Pages, familiar figures in Medieval society. Their appearance on playing cards may have been inspired by chess pieces; a game played in aristocratic circles in the 13th century, referred to in records of the time as *Quatuor Reges*, or The Four Kings, was once thought to be a card game but is now known to have been a form of chess.

In addition, most early Tarot cards had chequered backs, suggesting the design of a chess-board.

It has been said that the suit-signs of the lesser arcana—batons, cups, swords and coins—were devised to reflect the four main divisions of society in Medieval Europe: the nobility (swords); the clergy (cups); the merchants (coins); and the peasants (batons or clubs).

This is almost certainly a later rationalisation, for these four symbols are not peculiar to the Tarot alone. In fact, their history can be traced back many centuries.

The four Grail Hallows

The stories of the Holy Grail, which were first popularised in the Latin prose of Geoffrey of Monmouth shortly after 1130, speak of four sacred objects, or "Grail Hallows". The precise nature of these devices differs from one version of the legend to another, but they are often described thus:

The first was the Grail itself, identified with the cup used by Christ at the Last Supper, which was said to dispense whatever food was most desired.

The second was the "Sword of the Spirit", the legendary sword wielded by King David in the Old Testament.

The third was the sacred lance, said to be the lance of Longinus, the Roman soldier who pierced Christ's side on the cross.

The fourth was the platter from which Christ and his disciples ate the Paschal Lamb.

The grail and the platter are, of course, analogous to the chalice and paten used in the Catholic mass, but the four symbols together are pre-Christian in origin.

The sources of the Grail legends are, like the Tarot, many and divergent, but they were in part the Christian reworking of a Celtic mythological cycle which originated in Ireland and spread into Wales and parts of Cornwall.[11]

The Norman Conquest of Britain had brought French culture as far west as Wales, and in the second half of the 12th century the Arthurian legends were translated into French. These were followed by the first, though unfinished French version of the Grail cycle, the *Conte del Graal*, composed by Chrétien de Troyes in 1190.

The four Grail Hallows were in part descendents of the Four Treasures of Ireland, the magical emblems of the *Tuatha dé Danaan*, or people of the goddess Danu, who were the gods of the Celts in pre-Christian Ireland.[12]

These four treasures were:

(1) The cauldron of The Dagda. The Dagda was *Eochaid Ollathair*, Father of All. He was thought of as nourisher of the people, because his cauldron could never be emptied.

(2) The spear of Lug. Lug was a supremely versatile god, hence his title *Samildánach*, Many-skilled. He fought with the spear and sling, both weapons which require dexterity.

(3) The sword of Nuada. Nuada was king of the *Tuatha*, and his sword was said to be so powerful that no enemy could escape it once it had been unsheathed.

(4) The stone of Fál. This was the Stone of Sovereignty, which cried out loud when trodden on by the lawful King of Ireland.

How these four ancient and sacred symbols, the Four Treasures of Ireland, or Grail Hallows, came to be used as suit-marks on playing cards (or if indeed there is any connection between them) is a mystery, but it can be seen that the symbolism of the Tarot lesser arcana is not isolated.

The Arthurian romances, like the Gnostic religions, were at heart concerned with man's quest for wisdom, psychic growth, and ultimate spiritual emancipation. Their subject was the search of the individual for meaningful experience which would help him attain a greater degree of maturity, and a more satsifactory wholeness of personality and relationship with his environment.[13]

The Tarot symbolism of cup, baton, sword and coin cannot be restricted to one tradition only, any more than can the emblems of the major trumps. The quaternary of opposing yet complementary symbols is found in many places at many times, and the Tarot suits represent the coming together of several cultural streams.[14]

Perhaps the last word on the origin of Tarot cards should be left to one of the earliest writers to examine the subject. In his "Capitolo del Gioco della Primiera", published at Rome in 1526, Pietropaulo da San Chirico wrote: "We have but little certainty who was the inventor, or who, in the first instance, developed the game, nor is that little confirmed by authority to be relied on. Some say it was Lorenzo de Medici the Magnificent and relate I know not what tale of an Abbott: the which truly, for that the affair is not worth the trouble, and I cannot relate it, be it well or ill done, I have thus left to be sought by the more curious. Others will have it, that Ferdinand of Naples, he who so distinguished himself, was the inventor. Others Matthias, King of Hungary; many the Queen Isabella; some the Grand Seneschal. In short; because this observation is as superfluous as the first, we shall leave the search to those who are desirous of knowing how many barrels of wine Acestes gave to Aeneas; or what was the name of Anchises' nurse; and the like curiosities, worse than the Egg and the Chicken: for my part, were I asked, I should say that they ever were, and ever will be: and I am of the opinion that none of these found the cards, but that the cards found them."[15]

3

THE MEANING OF THE MAJOR TRUMPS

IN VIEW OF what is known of the Tarot cards it seems likely that they were devised to represent grades or stages in a system of initiation. In some ways Tarot imagery resembles that of alchemy, which, as C. G. Jung has shown, was for its more perceptive devotees a system of Hermetic training leading to spiritual enlightenment.

Western alchemy probably evolved in Egypt, in the Hellenistic civilisation of Alexandria, which was also an early stronghold of Gnosticism.[1] If this is so, then the alchemical treatises and the Tarot cards are both examples of the secret language of symbolism which initiates of all ages have devised to instruct their disciples and confound the profane.

These arcane doctrines have received much fresh scrutiny in modern times as a result of Jung's discovery that the works of the alchemists concealed a sophisticated system for the attainment of psychic integration which was remarkably similar to the stages of his own "process of individuation".[2]

Jung defined individuation as the expanding self-awareness of the individual and of society; an ordered process of psychic development leading to an increasing wholeness and "rounding out" of life.

The urge towards maturity can take two forms, he believed. First, there is the natural process of growth which takes place in every living thing, and which occurs in man without his conscious direction or control. Second, there can be a consciously directed programme of inner development which is stimulated by precise doctrines and practices.

The second kind of individuation process differs from the first in that the conscious mind monitors what is happening, and strives to manipulate the life-stream into channels which will further its own psychic development.

To take up the challenge of directed individuation requires courage and determination; it is an heroic adventure, the age-old quest of the hero which appears in every culture under the guise of myth and legend. Temptations will constantly be encountered, agonising choices frequently required, vigilance always called for.

The perils and rewards of this quest are surely what the Tarot is concerned with. Each of the twenty-two major trumps describes a stage in the journey of life which is crucial in some way. Only by solving the riddle which each card in turn presents can the way ahead be opened up and the development of the personality taken further.

According to Jung, the individuation process encompasses the whole of life, but falls naturally into two halves. The first half is concerned with the individual's relationship to the world outside himself; it is directed towards the development of the conscious mind and the stabilisation of the ego.

The second half reverses this process and confronts the ego with the depths of its own psyche, seeking to establish links with the inner self, the true centre of consciousness.

The two phases oppose one another, yet are complementary. The first half of life can be thought of as solar in nature, as it is outward-turning, active, positive, expansive. The second half is lunar in nature, being introspective, meditative, and passive in its relationship to the physical universe.[3]

If we examine the twenty-two Tarot trumps with this in mind, we find that they fall naturally into two groups, with The Wheel of Fortune significantly at the mid-point.

The turning-point between one half of life and the other is of critical importance; at the high-point of physical existence one is suddenly confronted with the inevitability of death. As Jung himself has said: "At the stroke of noon the descent begins. And the descent means the reversal of all the ideals and values that were cherished in the morning."[4]

The cards dealing with the first half of the life-cycle commence with the unnumbered card, The Fool, and end with The Wheel of Fortune.

The Fool can be seen as the newly born child entering the world, pure, innocent, and unaware of itself as a separate entity; it is still enveloped in the folds of the unconscious.

The second card, The Magician, symbolises the dawning of self-awareness and the emergence of the individual ego. Man is shown wielding the magical weapons of consciousness, with which he will conquer the world.

The next four cards, The High Priestess, The Empress, The Emperor, and The High Priest, allude to the four powers that the infant ego is subject to: male and female, material and spiritual. These cards might also be said to refer to the channels through which the individual relates to his surroundings; the four Jungian "functions": Intuition, Feeling, Sensation, and Thought.

Card VI, The Lovers, indicates the first decisive choice in life, the rejection in adolescence of one's family in favour of a mate. With this card the individual becomes responsible for his actions, and thus for his destiny.

Next we see The Chariot, signifying the need for successful adaptation to the laws of society, and the construction of a safe "vehicle", or persona, in which to proceed through the world.

Justice coincides with the onset of physical maturity, and indicates that until now the individual's development has been one-sided, the conscious aspect having been developed at the expense of the unconscious. The time has come when the balance must be redressed if psychic stagnation is to be avoided. Justice is the voice of conscience.

The Hermit describes the process of self-examination which will follow if the promptings of conscience are heeded. The broad highway travelled by the Charioteer has come to an end, and a new and narrower path must now be found.

Then we arrive at The Wheel of Fortune, the mid-point of life, the stage at which the peak is passed and the descent begins.

In the next card, the Hermit has successfully reorientated himself by realising that his apparently insurmountable difficulties are common to all mankind. The insight that his sufferings are not peculiar to him alone gives him the detachment necessary to subdue the fears within, as the woman in the card Fortitude is seen

41

overcoming the lion. Only by a fearless confrontation can the primeval forces of the unconscious be disarmed.

The Hanged Man symbolises the reversal of values and aims which should take place during the second half of life. Courage is needed to renounce the past in favour of an uncertain future. But the sacrifice must be made for psychic progress to continue.

The next card, Death, is sometimes entitled Transformation, as it points to a transformation of consciousness which must now take place. The ego must be transcended; the death of the old self must be sought in order that the energy locked within it might be released and directed towards the maturation of the higher self.

Temperance reveals that the sacrifice of the demands of the ego has resulted in a renewal of contact with the powers of life. The greatest challenge of the quest, the descent into the underworld in search of that which was lost, has ended in victory; consciousness is in communion with the unconscious, and the imbalance shown earlier by Justice is being redressed.

The Devil indicates that the dangers of the journey are not yet over, however. The forces of the unconscious have been released, and the seeker must either submit to the mindless powers of instinct, or else absorb and transmute them into a higher and positive form.

The reverse side of The Devil, Satan or the demiurge, is the glorious angel Lucifer, the light-bringer. The next card, The Tower, graphically describes the gift of Lucifer. His light is the fire of enlightenment which descends like a flash of lightning, destroying everything in its path which is not compatible with its own nature. It is the surge of power which is felt when the psychological blocks between the lower and higher selves are removed, and the light of God irradiates the personality.

The Star is a symbol of higher consciousness, the Evening Star which will act as a guide during the darkness which must follow the blinding brilliance of the divine lightning-bolt.

The Moon symbolises the final great trial which must be gone through, the dark night of the soul which follows the withdrawal of the inward light, and everything is seen as illusion. The test here is one of faith.

The Sun represents the reconciliation of the opposites, the

coming together of the mortal and immortal selves. This card is analogous to the marriage of the royal brother and sister in alchemy. The night is past and a new day is dawning.

Judgement shows the rebirth of the integrated self, therefore figures are seen rising from the dead on the Day of Judgement.

The World is a mandala, the androgynous figure dancing within an encircling wreath being a symbol of psychic wholeness which expresses in its symmetry the complete order and fulfilment of the mature psyche.

It can also be seen as a representation of a child in the womb, in which case it leads naturally on to the card at the beginning of the sequence, the Fool, the newborn child commencing its journey through life. This would accord well with the Gnostic doctrines regarding reincarnation and the succession of lives leading on to higher and still higher attainment.

If the major arcana of the Tarot pack illustrates twenty-two important stages in the path of life, then each card can be interpreted at several levels. It can point to important principles and forces operating in the world; it can unveil significant processes in the expansion of mystical consciousness; it can indicate the emergence of as yet unevolved aspects of personality, and when reversed, it can warn of physical or psychic pitfalls which may be encountered.

The Tarot speaks in the language of symbols, the language of the unconscious, and when approached in the right manner it may open doors into the hidden reaches of the soul.

The mysterious beauty of the cards provides a stimulus that awakens one's intuitive faculties, leading on to an understanding which lies outside the scope of the intellect. As the mind explores the Tarot images it uncovers meanings and significances which cannot be fully defined or brought completely into the light of reason.

The Tarot links the world of man with the world of the spirit, binding together all levels of reality and opening inner doors which were hitherto closed. A large part of the enduring value of these cards lies in the fact that their imagery cannot be fitted into any hard and fast dogma; they can never be fully comprehended and therefore offer new and original insights to everyone who studies them.

The cards are vehicles for the powers of life, the archetypal contents of the unconscious. Thoughtful meditation on their enigmatic designs can lead to a stirring of the creative forces of the psyche, an inward illumination which not only expands the confines of the conscious mind but also serves to activate the hidden faculties of the unconscious.

In the illustration (frontispiece) you will see the twenty-two cards of the greater arcana laid out in the form of a horizontal figure eight. This shape, an ancient symbol of eternity, occurs regularly in early Tarot packs—it can be seen in the hats worn by The Magician and the young woman in Fortitude, and in the headgear of several of the court card figures. It is shown in the design of minor cards such as the 2 of Coins, and in the hour-glass held in some packs by The Hermit. The cards are shown arranged in this pattern because, though it is perhaps arbitrary, it illustrates the overall plan of the cards in a striking way.

Starting with The Fool, follow the cards round in sequence. You will see that the first ten cards point outwards, away from the centre. These are the cards referring to the first, solar half of life, when the growing personality is concerned with confronting and relating to the world outside itself.

The Wheel of Fortune lies at the junction of the two circles, indicating the mid-point of life when attention is turned inwards. The following ten cards all point inwards, showing the lunar, introverted nature of the second half of the individuation process.

The final card, The World, lies like The Wheel of Fortune at the junction of the two circles, indicating the ending of one life-cycle and the commencement of the next.

This arrangement of the cards undoubtedly brings strange parallels and correspondences between them to light. For example, compare each card in one circle with its opposite number in the other circle.

The High Priest on the right corresponds to The Devil on the left. Each card depicts an enthroned male figure who has two devotees at his feet. The High Priest can be said to represent the outer form of religious observance, dogma and the rule of rational ecclesiastical law, whilst The Devil represents the inward domination of instincts and basic animal drives.

44

The Emperor represents the foundation of a material empire based on the values of human society; his opposite number is The Tower, symbol of the destruction of such edifices by the forces of the unconscious.

The High Priestess is the lunar Goddess of intuitive wisdom, a positive aspect of the anima. The opposing card is The Moon, the weaver of delusion, the negative anima.

The Chariot shows the success and optimism of youth, which is negated by the card complementing it, Death.

The two cards which overlap at the centre of the spread are striking in their similarity. The Wheel of Fortune and The World are both mandala-like designs. But the figures depicted on the first card are less than human, and are outside the wheel, whilst on the second card the single figure is more than human, and has attained a central position on the card, the hub of the wheel.

Many such affinities and counterpoises become apparent when the cards are studied and compared. As stated earlier, the Tarot pack is both complex and subtle in its allusions and correspondences, and the interpretations given here are just some of the possibilities inherent in the cards.

In the next chapter you will find each of the twenty-two cards illustrated separately, with a fuller commentary appended to each one.

4

THE MAJOR ARCANA

EACH OF THE twenty-two cards of the Tarot major trumps contains a wealth of symbolism and possible meanings. This chapter
is not intended to analyse all the possible variations, but it may
throw light on some of the more obvious allusions.

For example, most of the cards contain references to either
Classical myth and legend or else Biblical imagery. Some seem to
be the product of specifically Medieval concepts, whilst others have
parallels in other cultures at other times. A few cards may refer to
contemporary events or personages, or include alchemical or
heretical religious symbols.

Taken in sequence the cards can certainly be interpreted psychologically in terms of man's quest for enlightenment; when reversed
they can warn of perils and obstacles on the path.

Finally, each card has assigned to it certain meanings which are
used in the art of Tarot divination. The technique of divination
will be found later in the book, in chapter 8, but the meanings of
the major trumps are given here because in many cases they throw
extra light on their significance.

Variations in symbolism which do not appear in the drawings
illustrating this chapter (e.g. The Magician's floppy-brimmed hat)
will generally be found in the designs following page 27.

THE FOOL

THE FOOL

Traditionally this card is either unnumbered, or else, occasionally, is numbered zero. It depicts a man dressed as a court jester. The Jester or Fool was a familiar figure in Medieval and Renaissance Europe; although some Jesters were merely hunchbacks, dwarfs or cretins, many were highly gifted acrobats, singers and dancers who held a special position at court.

The Fool was often allowed to satirise his masters or play outrageous tricks which ordinary men dared not emulate. A particularly gifted Fool might sometimes gain a reputation which extended far beyond the confines of his master's realm, and occasionally one would achieve an international reputation as an entertainer and be able to travel far and wide, offering his services to those kings, princes and barons who could afford his fees.

The Fool depicted on the Tarot card, however, does not seem to have attained such eminence.

In many old packs his clothes are ragged and he is being

attacked by a dog that tears at his legs as he marches along. He carries a bag slung over his shoulder on the end of a stick, and grasps a sturdy staff in one hand. The bag may have originally represented an inflated pig's bladder, a primitive balloon which was part of the Jester's stock-in-trade.

Sometimes he is shown following a brightly coloured butterfly or insect that flutters before his face, in which case the bag may really be a butterfly net in which he hopes to catch his prey.

The archetype of the wise Fool is one that is found in many cultures in all parts of the world. His lack of experience in the ways of society is seen on the surface to be a disadvantage, but in reality it ensures that his mind is not closed to unusual experiences that are denied to ordinary men.

He is the vagabond who exists on the fringe of organised life, going his own way, ignoring the rules and taboos with which men seek to contain him. He is the madman who carries within him the seeds of genius, the one who is despised by society yet who is the catalyst which will transform that society.

The Fool is the Green Man, the harbinger of a new cycle of existence, the herald of new life and fresh beginnings. He can be seen as the innocent spirit about to embark on physical incarnation; the young child who has yet to learn of the perils in the world; or as the seeker after enlightenment chasing the elusive butterfly of intuition in the hope that it will lead him to the mysteries.

The mood is joyous and carefree, yet hints of pitfalls and trials just ahead.

He represents the chaos before reason, the pure impulse that is neither good nor evil. Symbolically the Fool can be said to be both the beginning and the end, therefore he is not limited by being assigned a number, and can appear at the beginning or the end of the twenty-two card sequence.

When he appears, as here, at the beginning, he can be interpreted psychologically as representing the newly-born child which is not yet aware of itself as a separate entity. He is not yet an individual, and therefore is not responsible for his actions as an individual.

He is shown setting out on his journey into life entranced by the bright butterfly of sensory experience and heedless of all warnings about the fall into the bondage of matter that lies just ahead.

His bag contains those elusive memories of what he is leaving behind, memories that will urge him ever onwards in his search to recover what he is about to lose—his primeval innocence.

In some Tarot packs he is seen to carry a small flower loosely in one hand; this is his soul, the fragment of divinity which he will bear with him through all the trials ahead.

The negative aspect of the Fool reveals the Joker, who chases in pursuit of extravagant amusements, heedless of the chaos and anarchy he leaves in his wake. The heady joy of the moment is his only concern.

Divinatory meanings:

Upright: Indicates an influence which is unexpected and unplanned, but which exerts a powerful force on the matter in hand. It is a challenge that can transform the situation in the querent's favour if properly handled. It indicates that an important decision or choice will have to be made. If this card is well placed, flanked by fortune cards, then a wise decision will be made, and perseverance will bring its rewards. If badly placed, flanked by unfortunate cards, warning is given of impending error. The Fool can also indicate the imminent start of a new cycle of destiny, and can refer to a type of person—the creative dreamer.

Reversed: Foretells of major problems arising from reckless, impulsive action.

THE MAGICIAN

I THE MAGICIAN

A young man wearing a distinctive hat with a large floppy brim stands behind a table on which are arranged a variety of instruments or tools. In some packs these are seen to be the suit-signs of the Tarot minor arcana—the cup, baton, sword and coin—whilst in other packs they are an odd assortment of shoe-maker's tools. The card has been variously entitled the Magician, the Minstrel, the Conjurer, or the Cobbler.

Probably he was originally meant to represent the travelling showman, an entertainer like the Fool, who moved from town to town and village to village, either alone or with a troop of actors and musicians, giving shows, telling fortunes, and selling quack remedies. Often such men, who were viewed with suspicion by established authorities and often lived a precarious existence, would be the means by which unorthodox teachings or heretical ideas would be transmitted abroad.

This character, half mountebank and half wise man, was chosen by the creators of the Tarot sequence to lead the numbered cards. He is assigned the number one, the number of positive action, individuality and creativity. The Magician is forceful and self-confident, and stands alone.

He can perhaps be seen as Prometheus, grasping the hollow fennel stalk in which he brought down the gift of fire from Heaven after stealing it from the Gods. The character of Promethus as depicted in the Greek myths seems very like that of the Tarot Magician; he was quick-witted and wily, like the gods Hermes and Loki, or the American Indian folk-hero Coyote, and was also strong-willed and self-assured, as shown in his defiance of Zeus.

Psychologically the myth of Prometheus can be said to refer to the time when man first attained self-consciousness, "stealing" it from the unconscious and thus taking upon himself one of the attributes of divinity.

In so doing he also assumed the responsibilities of Godhood; he is now responsible for his actions. But in taking possession of the world he has lost sight of his soul. The light of the ego obscures the softer radiance of the spirit.

The rest of the Tarot cycle will be seen to display the perils and temptations that he must face on the long quest to rediscover what he has lost, carrying the sacred fire of consciousness with him as he goes.

Following on from the Fool, the Magician signifies the first stage of conscious existence, the emerging self-awareness of the child and the beginning of his journey through life. His first task will be to learn how to live in his environment; he must come to wield his elemental weapons—his physical senses—with power and authority before he can proceed.

Traditionally the Magician is the adept who has brought all facets of his being into conscious equilibrium, from the physical to the divine, and is therefore able to manifest divine power on the material plane. The sceptre he holds on high represents his flaming will, with which he controls the Four Elements—symbolised by the four devices that lie on the altar before him—the sword (air), the cup (water), the baton (fire) and the coin (earth).

The symbol above his head signifies the presence of the Holy Spirit, therefore his inspiration is seen to emanate from his own true Self, the spark of divinity within him. He acts with supreme confidence, knowing that whatever he wills must be in accordance with the Universal Will. He is the conscious link between the world of the Spirit and the world of man.

The Magician's inner garments are white to signify his inward purity and equilibrium; his outer robe and girdle are scarlet to show the fire of his purposeful activity. The lilies around his feet symbolise his aspiration, the roses his achievement.

He is the teacher who appears when the pupil is ready, the master of wisdom who will instruct the Fool in the hidden ways of the soul.

In mundane terms he is the man who uses his intellect and energy to explore and transform the world around himself, who is not satisfied with things the way they are but must ceaselessly search for meanings and alternatives.

Being unable to accept the explanations that are given him concerning the nature and goal of life, he must strive to uncover the secrets of existence for himself. In this aspect he is the hero who has embarked on the quest for wisdom, the seeker at the door of the hidden temple.

When reversed, the Magician becomes the Juggler, the trickster who conjures with life, delighting to observe the effect his clever sleight-of-hand has on lesser mortals. The object of his quest is not then wisdom, but power. If he succeeds in invoking real elemental forces, then he becomes a wizard—the instrument of those demonic powers he sought to control.

Divinatory meanings:

Upright: Points to strength of will, the expansion of the personality, a willingness to face risks, initiative that will lead to success and triumph. Also adaptability and versatility, diplomacy and self-confidence. Can indicate the commencement of an important new cycle in the querent's affairs.

Reversed: Weakness of will, failure of nerve, timidity and hesitation resulting in further problems; an inability to face reality.

II

THE PAPESS

II THE PAPESS

The Female Pope, or High Priestess, is depicted as a wise woman dressed in elaborate robes and heavy crown similar to those of the Pope. She holds an open book or a scroll in her lap and a veil or curtain is seen to hang behind her. On some examples of this card she is shown sitting between two pillars.

The legend of the Papess seems to have first appeared in Europe around the end of the twelfth century and became increasingly well known from then until it reached its peak of popularity at the time of the Reformation.

According to the story, she was a native of the town of Mainz in Germany who fell in love with an Englishman and, disguised as a boy, travelled with him to Athens and then Rome, studying there under the name Johannes Angelicus.

By reason of her talent and brilliance she eventually rose to the Papal chair, taking the name John VIII. She was believed to have reigned successfully from 854 to 856, between the Popes Leo IV and Benedict III, but unfortunately became pregnant and died near the Coliseum whilst giving birth to a child during a solemn procession.

This curious tale was without foundation,[1] and was probably compounded from half-remembered pagan myth allied to heretical speculation. In the Cathari and other Medieval sects women are known to have been admitted to the highest officiating positions.

In the Tarot sequence the Female Pope is assigned the number two, which symbolises counterpoise, relativity, the dualism of the "pairs of opposites" that develop from the number one, or unity. It represents the interaction of poles which gives rise to manifestation, and in the human sphere signifies man's experience of individual existence, as a separate ego divorced from the world around him. It is the number of time, as opposed to timelessness, creation as opposed to the creator, the reflected light of the moon as opposed to the direct light of the sun.

Following from this, the Female Pope can be seen as a linear descendant of the High Priestesses of antiquity, the embodiment of the lunar goddesses of combination and procreation.

The appearance of the Female Pope in some Tarot packs resembles that of the Egyptian goddess Isis, or the lunar diety Hathor. Hathor was the guide to a secret land—the land of the dead, hence her title Queen of the West. Her protection was invoked on behalf of the dead and the dying. In the great temple of Hathor at Denderah was to be found a shrine dedicated to the dog-star Sothis, or Sirius, and the dog, too, is traditionally a guide to the land of the dead. Curiously, one of the esoteric titles of the Female Pope is "Priestess of the Silver Star".

It has been said of her that she is "the great feminine force controlling the very source of life, gathering into herself all the energising forces and holding them in solution until the time of release."[2] Therefore she is depicted sitting between the twin pillars of positive and negative power upon which the universe is founded, absorbing and unifying the opposing energies.

She is the passive link between the physical and spiritual planes; through her, it is said, God can be realised in the heart of man, hence her title "The Indwelling Glory".

As the unspoken words of initiation can only be heard by the intuition, the Fool's first task is to learn the secret language of the High Priestess so that he might at length read the words in her book of wisdom. The book or scroll she holds in her lap represents the mysteries of the hidden temple of which she is the guardian.

In Qabalistic language she is said to be the Shekhinah, the Indwelling Glory that descends to irradiate the temple when the two pillars are brought into perfect equilibrium; she is the visible reflection of the divine radiance upon which no man can look and live. As such she is the bringer of inspiration and the source of all intuitory knowledge, the channel whereby the divine is made manifest on earth.

Psychologically, she symbolises one of the bridges linking the twin pillars of the conscious and unconscious minds, the inspirer of dreams and visions that reveal the continuance of life beyond conscious boundaries.

The veil behind her hides a door that gives entrance into the inner worlds of the psyche; it allows the conscious mind to pass within and enables the powers of the unconscious to manifest themselves without. Creative inspiration and intuitive revelation are two of the forces which can only flow when the way is open.

To those who are prepared she reveals herself as the Lady of Light who points out the concealed path by the beams of her gentle lunar radiance, and gives freely her patronage and protection. Under this aspect she is Divine Inspiration—Sophia, the Gnostic goddess of wisdom.

The High Priestess can also be seen as one aspect of the feminine element within man, the Anima. This is a primeval image contained in the masculine unconscious which in no way represents any single woman, yet which will be projected on to several women in the course of a lifetime, endowing them for a space with a magic that can either inspire or lead to destruction.

The negative aspect of this image is revealed when the reality and potency of the feminine element within is unrecognised or misunderstood. In this guise the Goddess of Wisdom becomes the *femme fatale*; Hecate, Queen of the Dark of the Moon, Lilith, Ruler of Demons, the weaver of illusions who destroys her lovers.

Divinatory meanings:

Upright: The revealing of hidden things which bring strength and hope. Intuitive insight into problems which will suggest new solutions. This card can indicate the influence of a woman who is wise or inspired. To the artist or innovator she represents the source of creative talent.

Reversed: Warns against difficulties arising from emotional instability. In a man's spread it can symbolise the bad influence of a woman on him, one by whom he is emotionally enslaved. Also indicates problems resulting from lack of foresight or reluctance to take sound advice.

III THE EMPRESS

Here we see a matronly woman seated out of doors. She is crowned and carries a sceptre in one hand. A shield emblazoned with an eagle is also shown, sometimes cradled in her arm, other times resting by her foot. She looks prosperous and sedate.

Whether or not this image incorporates any historical allusions is not known, although it is possible that she was modelled on one of the famous Empresses of Byzantium, or on one of the members of the Hohenstaufen dynasty which exerted a powerful influence on the course of Medieval history.

The Empress is assigned the number three, the number of synthesis and harmony. It represents the resolving of the tension created by duality through the birth of a third, unifying principle.

Three is therefore the number of childbirth, new life, fecundation and material productivity. Whereas two indicates the extension of time from the past to the future, three adds the dimension of space, symbolising the creation of phenomena in time.

The Empress is the great Mother Goddess, the source of all living things. She embodies the super-abundant creative forces of nature, together with the benign feminine wisdom of the Queen of Life. Her concerns are essentially those of the physical plane. She is the ruler of paradise on earth, and her pregnant figure reveals her role as guardian of childbirth and motherhood.

She is the descendant of earth goddesses such as the Greek Demeter or the Sumerian Ishtar, deities which probably preceded the masculine-orientated pantheons of the Classical world. They were the patronesses of Mystery cults such as that of Eleusis, at which the sacred dramas of death and the renewal of life were played out for the benefit of initiates. Eleusis was dedicated to the myth of the corn-goddess Demeter and her daughter Persephone, who was carried off to the underworld as the bride of Hades or Pluto, only to be allowed to return to the upper regions for eight months of the year in order that summer might return and life continue.

Demeter and Persephone were the goddesses of life and death, suggesting a parallel with the Tarot images of The Empress and The Papess, the light and dark sides of creation.

The power of the Empress is passive, feminine, not active intellectual control as exercised by the Magician. Her weapons are emotion and feeling, not thought.

In the spiritual sphere she represents that faith which springs from the comfort of material things and an emotional appreciation of the workings of nature. She brings about spiritual awakening through devotion to physical work and creation, and like the Papess she functions as one of the paths that lead to deeper levels of awareness.

This aspect of the Empress is shown by her shield bearing the device of an eagle. The eagle is the soul enthroned in nature.

Here the seeker after wisdom encounters his second challenge. He must learn to discern the workings of heaven in the things of earth, and come to realise that the material universe is nothing less than the luminous garment of the divine.

In the mundane world she represents feeling. The function of feeling in this sense refers to a kind of judgement—not judgement in the sense of a conclusion reached by a process of thought, but rather an intuitive sorting out and applying of values to things. This ability is generally more highly developed in women than in men, although some men do exhibit it in an advanced form.

The Empress is the ultimate feeling type, who rules her complex realm by a delicately balanced discrimination based on her sense of values. The woman who has a developed sense of feeling reveals it in a similar manner; she is a fair and sympathetic mother, dedicated to the well-being of her family, and she makes a warm and helpful member of the community. She is adept at handling people and getting the best out of them, and reveals a deep understanding of their problems and difficulties.

The Empress can also manifest through the male sex. If her gifts are allowed to enrich the conscious mind like the golden fruits of the cornucopia she reveals herself as the beautiful Lady who inspires her worshippers with devotion to her Ideal, or whose image arouses chivalrous thoughts in the hearts of men.

Like the Papess, the negative aspect of the Empress is often revealed through the male sex. The young man's first experience of women is in the person of his mother, and he focuses upon her all the attributes of the Empress. In some cases this initial projection is so powerful that it lingers thoughout life, colouring and distorting all subsequent relations with women and imprisoning the mind in an emotional strait-jacket that stunts its proper growth. Under this aspect the Empress becomes Kali, the dark goddess who consumes her own children.

Divinatory meanings:

Upright: Fertility, abundance, fruitfulness, motherhood. Indicates domestic stability, sympathetic honesty, maternal care and protection. Comfort or inspiration gained through contact with nature. Reassurance and a sense of security obtained through the pleasures of the senses. Also a symbol of growth; the establishment of a firm foundation for future progress.

Reversed: Domestic upheaval, maternal tyranny or over-protectiveness. Sterility or an unwanted pregnancy. A sense of the universe as either impersonal or malevolent. Psychic alienation. Poverty.

THE EMPEROR

IV THE EMPEROR

The Emperor is depicted sitting on a throne in the open air. He wears a crown, and in some Tarot packs a suit of armour. He carries a sceptre, and by his side, or engraved on his throne, is a shield bearing the device of an eagle.

This card is numbered four in the sequence. Four is the number of concrete organisation, the "four-square" logic of mundane laws. It indicates reason, will-power, and the world of mankind on the earth.

The Emperor is the consort of the Empress. He too represents creation, but the creation of the will, not the feelings. He symbolises power rather than love.

Mythologically he is a descendant of father-figures such as the Greek god Uranus, lord of the sky whose mating with his consort Mother Earth united the two halves of the cosmic egg and gave birth to the universe out of chaos.

He is the symbol of the warlike patriarchal societies which

superseded the primitive agricultural cultures of the Great Mother.

Historically he may be likened to the Byzantine Emperors, or the Hohenstaufen Emperor Frederick II who was one of the dominant figures of Europe in the first half of the 13th century.

The sceptre he grasps is the symbol of his masculine potency, the creative energy with which he builds and sustains his empire. The golden orb indicates his rational understanding of the laws of the physical plane, that enables him to organise the world around himself and formulate rules for other men to live by. The cubic throne on which he sits represents his dominion over brute force and unorganised matter.

He wears a heavy crown in token of his worldly authority and triumph on the material plane, but the barren land in which he sits suggests the sterility of a masculine world founded solely on power, excluding the gentler feminine virtues exemplified by his mate, the Empress.

The significance of the Emperor in the spiritual world is indicated by the device engraved on his throne or shield. The eagle is said to symbolise the human soul purified by discipline and controlled will-power. Only by battling through the adversities of life and triumphing over circumstances can the spirit achieve freedom.

In the mundane world the Emperor is he who by the intelligent use of his own resources has triumphed over physical restrictions. He has mastered the world around himself by constant effort and untiring tenacity. He bases all his decisions on what his senses tell him; every experience is taken at its face value and he is very much the product of his environment.

His great reliance on tangible facts and his measured manner of acting on them makes him the focus of general admiration, and he is believed to be a logical and admirably balanced character who can be trusted to do the right thing at the right time.

But sense impressions are received by the brain in a random fashion, and the importance given to any one impression at a given moment depends on many factors. Thus the Emperor operates largely on the impulse of the moment and soon steps out of his depth when called upon to deal with larger issues that require subtler qualities.

As the male child endows his mother with the attributes of the Empress, the female child often sees her father as the Emperor. Like that of the mother, the father-image is an immensely powerful figure who can influence a woman's entire life. Many women go through life doing things they think father would have approved of, voicing opinions father would have held, and attributing all this to "just sound common sense".

The Emperor as father-figure does have a positive side, though: he can give a woman some of the powerful masculine qualities necessary in the battle of life—a strong will, courage, and fearlessness. On the one hand he can be an unbending tyrant, on the other a powerful ally. But he must be relied on for his strength, and not for his judgement.

Divinatory meanings:

Upright: Will-power, self-control, conquest, authority and ambition. Knowledge acquired through experience, creative energy, vigour, all martial qualities. A great person, with influence to put at the disposal of the querent.

Reversed: Immaturity or weakness, subservience to those in authority, loss of an influential position, failure of ambition.

THE POPE

V THE POPE

The figure of a Pope is seen, robed and crowned. With one hand he blesses the two tonsured priests who kneel before him, whilst in the other hand he holds a triple-tiered cross. Behind him are two pillars. The two clerics are either tonsured, or else are wearing large-brimmed circular hats. In some Tarot packs the Pope is bearded, in others clean-shaven.

The Pope was of course a familiar figure in the society of the Middle Ages, but the creators of the Tarot images must have been at some risk in taking the liberty of depicting him on one of their cards, unless the pack was designed at a time when the Papacy was absent from Italy.

After Pope Boniface VIII had been captured at Anagni in 1302 by the forces of Philip IV of France, the Papal seat was removed to Avignon, where it remained until 1378.

Does the figure shown here represent a particular Pope—perhaps looking back to the famous Innocent III, whose pontificate ran from 1198 to 1216, and whose alliance with the Emperor Frederick II of Germany resulted in some extraordinary political successes—or is he simply a symbol of ecclesiastical authority, or even a prudently disguised non-Christian priest? The identity of the Tarot Pope has never been established, though the last alternative seems most likely.

In discussing the symbolical role of the Pope we are on safer ground. He is assigned the number five in the Tarot sequence, the number of mental inspiration, creative thought, moral law and intellectual synthesis. It represents the "rounding-out" of life, the four cardinal points of spatial organisation united in a common centre.

Just as the Emperor is the consort of the Empress, the Pope is the masculine counterpart of the Papess. Like the Roman Catholic Pontiff, whose figure he resembles, he is the representative of God on earth, the shepherd of his flock who holds for them the keys that unlock the gates of Heaven and Hell. The title Pontiff comes from the Latin *pontifex*, meaning bridge-maker, and the Tarot Pope is the fourth major bridge linking the outer world of the senses to the inner world of the spirit.

He is the upholder of orthodox religion and an accepted code of behaviour within society. The pillars behind him are the supports of the established church of which he is the guardian and spokesman. He instructs his people in the world concerning that which lies beyond it. His teachings are practical and sensible, and his honesty is indicated by his wearing gloves.

The following words of Jung can be aptly applied to this Tarot character: "He is the 'informing spirit' who initiates the dreamer into the meaning of life and explains its secrets according to the teachings of old. He is a transmitter of the traditional wisdom."[3]

His golden triple-tiered crown is the symbol of his wisdom and his understanding of the physical, emotional and mental spheres. The crook which appears in some packs is the sign of his ecclesiastical authority—he is the spiritual mentor, or Good Shepherd. The priests kneeling at his feet to receive his blessing and instruction represent the contemplative and the active.

The Pope's capacity for deep and profound thought can produce fresh ideas and original insights, even though these will be firmly bound within a traditional framework. Through his inspiration man's links with God are constantly being renewed and re-interpreted, and thus every age receives its own signposts freshly painted and pointing out the way.

Interpreted mundanely, the Pope represents the man who likes his world to be neat, tidy and carefully labelled. He lives his life according to a carefully worked out formula, and holds a hearty dislike of those who muddle along with no clear end in view.

He tends to think that the way that is right for him is equally right for everyone else, and feels it his duty to point this out to them. His attitude of moral superiority can make him impossible to live with. His philosophy may contain much that is good and progressive, but he may lack warmth, spontaneity and common humanity.

In his negative aspect the Pope can also be the intellectual oppressor, the seeker out of heresies and deviations from accepted dogma. Conversely he can himself become the teacher of false doctrines, who fosters superstition and fear of the unknown.

Divinatory meanings:

Upright: Good counsel, advice, exposition, teaching. A giver of wisdom or enlightenment, the revealer of that which is hidden. Freedom through knowledge, inspirational help, the comfort of religion.

Reversed: Misinformation, misrepresentation, distortion of the truth, power achieved through the withholding of information. Slander, propaganda. Bad advice.

VI

THE LOVERS

VI THE LOVERS

Here we see a young man flanked by two women. Each of the women seems to be trying to incline him in her direction, but he stands undecided between them. Above the group flies a winged Cupid, aiming his arrow at those beneath him.

The legend of Cupid and Psyche given in the *Golden Ass* of Apuleius became very widely known in the Middle Ages mainly through the writings of Boccaccio (1313–1375). So it is not surprising to find Cupid depicted in the Tarot pack.

This fat winged child of sentimental legend was a descendant of the early Greek god Eros, ruler of the procreative power of the universe. The god of love was not originally the patron of romantic dalliance but an irrepressible cosmic force, the primeval urge to create order out of chaos, the instrument of destiny.

His appearance on the Tarot card the Lovers reveals that a fateful conflict is being resolved. This card is number six in the sequence and six, like two, is a number signifying tension and ambivalence. Traditionally it is associated with the six days of creation recorded in Genesis, and is therefore also linked with ideas of advancement and evolution.

The Lovers symbolises the first decision which must be made unaided by the traveller on his journey through life. The youth is caught in the dilemma of having to choose between loyalty to his mother and desire for his beloved, between traditional authority and independent action. This is an important stage in the development of individuality; the stage at which the personality becomes an entity separate and apart from its origins.

The card contains a paradox. Only by withdrawal from the influence and authority of the mother can the quest proceed and the treasure hard to attain, immortality, be won at last. But by attaining independence he also ensures the eventual ending of independence; by winning life he is also presented with the prospect of death.

In psychological terms, Eros gives the capacity to relate opposing principles in a manner that not only harmonises them but also results in a whole that is greater than its parts. The synthesising quality of Eros smooths over the anomalies and antagonisms between the lovers and opens the way to their eventual union.

He is shown here about to loose his arrow, the uniting arrow of love which is also the shaft that strikes a deadly wound. It gives new life, and brings death in its train.

In a more mundane interpretation the maiden represents the path of outward activity, in which self-reliance and a sense of dedication and purpose strengthens the traveller and helps him to carve a path through the tangle of doubts and fears that surround him.

The older woman then represents the easier way of dependence on familiar and established authority which is prepared to assume responsibility for the subject's welfare. She offers the comfort and protection of an established way in return for loyalty and obedience.

The seeker has reached the point at which the two ways are seen to be incompatible. He reluctantly accepts that he must sacrifice one in order to know the other, and his decision can no longer be delayed.

Unwittingly, he is about to be rescued from his dilemma by his own Higher Self: Eros, his Holy Guardian Angel, who, shooting forth his arrow of divine purpose, makes the choice for him.

Eros is destiny incarnate and the young man has not reached the stage at which his destiny is within his own control. He is the product of his past, and the forces that formed his past will decide the course of his future. Whichever path he chooses will be the right one for him at this time.

The negative aspect of this card shows the neurotic who, through his fear of independent life, and perhaps subconsciously the fear of death, is unable to leave his mother. In terms of the quest, he had fallen at the first hurdle and his progress is at an end. Only stagnation lies ahead.

When reversed, it shows he who vacillates between two courses of action, unable to decide which to choose and evading the issue until the pressure of events—whether physical or psychological—forces him one way or the other. Until this happens he wastes time and energy fruitlessly searching for a compromise, unable to give up either of the attractive alternatives before him.

Divinatory meanings:

Upright: A time of choice, the outcome of which is of crucial importance. Reliance on intuition rather than intellect is advised, on inspiration rather than reason. This card can indicate a flash of insight that resolves an apparently insoluble problem. Also a moral choice which depends on maturity and integrity for its outcome.

Reversed: Danger of a moral lapse, severe temptation placed in the querent's path. Inability to make an important choice through a desire to have the best of all worlds.

VII THE CHARIOT

VII THE CHARIOT

This card shows a young man riding in a richly canopied chariot pulled by two horses. He is crowned, carries a sceptre, and wears armour. He gives an impression of power and self-confidence.

The charioteer does not have any obvious mythological antecedents, although symbolically he may be akin to the god Helios, riding in the chariot of the sun, or to Apollo, the patron of life, light and healing. Apollo was the god who symbolised self-discipline, morality, and the rule of law, and whose priests at Delphi taught "know thyself".

In the Tarot sequence the charioteer is assigned the number seven, a prime number which signifies unity within complexity. It is a number of far-reaching symbolical significance: the seven Classical planets, the seven virtues and seven vices, the seven ages of man, the seven days of the week, the Seven Seals of the Book of Revelation. It arises out of the combination of the numbers three and four, therefore the crowned charioteer can be seen as the royal progeny of the Empress (card III) and Emperor (card IV).

Seven is the number of progress, self-expression and independent action. In terms of the Tarot cycle, the Chariot portrays the fate of he who has made the right choice when faced by the dilemma shown in the previous card, the Lovers. He has successfully transferred his attention from his mother to his beloved, and is therefore in control of the psychic energy within him rather than being dominated by it.

This fundamental psychic energy, or libido, is frequently symbolised by a horse; thus the charioteer is seen to have harnessed his animal instincts, which are now drawing him effortlessly along his way. His mastery being complete, he does not need reins to guide the beasts.

The warrior in his four-sided chariot is the individual travelling smoothly along the road through life, safe within the armour of his Persona.

In ancient times the persona was a name given to the mask worn by an actor, and in modern psychological terms too it is a mask; the mask of appearance worn by the ego.

Everyone learns at an early age to play a role in life; we gradually ease ourselves into a position in society that "fits" our personality as we see it. Adopting the dress and mannerisms of those we admire, we try to appear to others as we would wish them to see us.

The young child soon learns the type of behaviour expected of it by its elders, and reacts accordingly. As it grows, the gaps in its rather sketchy persona are speedily filled in and by the time it reaches adulthood, if all goes well, it is equipped with a well-made and well-fitting suit of psychic armour.

Some people do not wear an adequate or consistent persona, and somehow we feel uncomfortable in their presence. We never know quite how they will act or what they are going to say next, a difficulty which makes it harder for us to maintain our own mask, which is largely held in place by the consistency of the social structure surrounding us. This is one aspect of the negative side of The Chariot.

The other is the danger that the mask will become too tight or rigid, restricting the development of personality, and perhaps causing the ego to identify itself with its persona, forgetting that it is only a mask worn for convenience. Such identification is another of the pitfalls that can bring the journey to a premature close.

The crescent moons on the charioteer's shoulders signify his mastery over the fluctuating tides of Lunar (subjective) forces within him, whilst his golden armour is his protection against the Solar (objective) forces that surround him. His crown in some Tarot packs incorporates a five-pointed star, symbol of psychic equilibrium, and his sceptre represents the authority of his steadfast will.

In the material world the charioteer is he who has taught himself to control his bodily functions and concentrate all his faculties on a single goal. By the concentrated use of his trained intellect and his disciplined body he rides confidently through the obstacles placed before him by circumstances, and dictates his own path. His practical understanding of the laws governing society give him the expertise to manipulate them to his own advantage.

When reversed, he is the man of power and wealth who uses his material resources to ride rough-shod over those who would oppose his grandiose plans. He may believe himself to be an idealist, but his only answer to those who question his aims is oppression.

Divinatory meanings:

Upright: Success, triumph over the obstacles life throws in one's path. Secure progress, victory achieved through personal effort, the triumph of initiative. Not success which is inherited, or the product of fortune.

Reversed: One who rides rough-shod over others. Overbearing forcefulness, inattention to the rights of others, egocentricity, ruthlessness.

VIII JUSTICE

Here we see a stern woman seated on a throne, bearing in her right hand an upraised sword, and in her left hand a pair of scales. She wears an elaborate headdress.

The conventional figure of Justice depicted here is a familiar one. She is one of the four Virtues—the others being Temperance, Fortitude, and Prudence—which occur frequently in Medieval art. She is assigned the number eight in the Tarot sequence.

Eight was known as the number of Justice to the Greeks, because it is made up of equal divisions of even numbers, suggesting therefore balance and equanimity. Also, because of its shape, the Arabic number eight is a symbol of eternity, completion, and thus the workings of destiny. The eight-sided figure or octogon was thought to stand midway between the square, symbol of the world of space and time, and the circle, symbol of eternity. It is therefore the point of balance between the outer world of the body and the inner realm of the spirit.

This suggests a key to the significance of the Tarot card Justice. It indicates the next stage in the life of the individual. He has reached maturity, finding his place in the world and achieving a secure environment in which to bring up his family. He is the "man of the world" who has reaped the rewards of his past efforts in terms of prosperity and status. His early dreams have been fulfilled in as great a degree as is possible; he has reached the peak of success.

But in the moment of triumph, he feels that not all is as it should be. Looking back over his life he notes a feeling of dissatisfaction, a feeling of emptiness—almost as if his life was missing some essential ingredient.

Such feelings of lack or even guilt generally manifest in middle-age, when the body begins to age visibly, and the certainty of death assumes a personal reality.

Justice is the voice of conscience, the voice of the inner self which points out that so far the needs and aspirations of the conscious mind, the ego, have been served, whilst the urges of the unconscious have been largely ignored. The time has come when the balance must be redressed; life must take an entirely new direction if justice is to be done.

If the needs of the unconscious are suppressed, the conscious mind either becomes inflated, scurrying after the things of youth, or else often falls into a profound depression.

Only by accepting the challenge of the second half of life as eagerly as he accepted the first, only by gazing fearlessly forward rather than longingly back, can the sword of Justice be avoided.

Not that the challenge is one lightly to be met; the obstacles and perils of the inner way of the soul are equal to, if not greater than, those of the outer way of the world.

In the mundane world the figure of Justice points the moral that we must all be weighed in the balance and receive our just deserts. That despite the apparent unfairness and lack of balance in the normal order of things, the fundamental imbalance lies within us and not in the world outside.

If we would make the most of our destinies we must follow the rhythms of the universe or else be constantly beaten back like a swimmer battling against the tide. Ignorance of the law is no more excuse in the Court of Life than in the courts of men—the laws must be studied and obeyed if the penalties for transgressing them are to be avoided.

The negative aspect of Justice reveals the dangers that can arise when the law is either misapplied or applied too rigidly. Carrying out the "letter of the law" is a human failing which has resulted in much injustice. When placed in human hands the sword of Justice all too often obscures her scales, and the virtue of mercy is easily forgotten.

Divinatory meanings:

Upright: The act of judgement. Arbitration, agreements reached by negotiation, the vindication of truth and integrity. This can be a card either of hope or of fear, depending on the moral position of the querent.

Reversed: Injustice, lack of fair dealing, bias, prejudice. Legal tangles that delay the administration of the law. Complex and expensive law-suits.

IX

THE HERMIT

IX The Hermit

An old man moves slowly along a dim and stony road. He is dressed in garments resembling those of a monk. The way before him is poorly lighted by a lantern which he carries in his right hand, shielded by his sleeve from the force of the wind. His left hand grasps a heavy staff, around which, in some packs, is entwined a serpent. Although his cloak is hooded, the hood is thrown back and his head is bare.

This card is number nine in the Tarot sequence. Nine is important symbolically in that it is the last of the single numbers; after it we return to number one, or unity. The Hermit, therefore, signifies the final stage of the first half of the Tarot quest.

In some ways this card is analogous to the Fool. Here the seeker is again setting off on the first stage of a journey, alone and with little to guide or sustain him. But he is represented as a solitary old man, a hermit, trudging along a dark and lonely road, instead of a child skipping gaily through the morning sunlight.

The quest of the first half of life, the outward-turning, Solar phase, has reached its conclusion, and the scales of Justice have tipped in favour of the second quest, into the inward-turning, Lunar world of the unconscious.

The Hermit has taken heed of the voice of Justice, his own conscience, and is seeking for answers to the questions that plague him. He knows that a duty has been laid upon him and that he will be unable to rest until he has fulfilled his obligations, but the way ahead is dark and he has only the light of his own intuition to help him find the right path. All the wealth and wisdom of the outer world cannot assist him now, and so he goes forth into the night dressed in a simple robe and carrying only a staff to lean on. The serpent curled around the staff symbolises his own innate store of unconscious wisdom, which will help him surmount the obstacles ahead.

Jung has said: "Isolation by a secret results as a rule in an animation of the psychic atmosphere, as a substitute for loss of contact with other people. It causes an activation of the unconscious, and this produces something similar to the illusions and hallucinations that beset lonely wanderers in the desert, seafarers, and saints. ... As a substitute for the normal animation of the environment, an illusory reality rises up in which weird ghostly shadows flit about in place of people."[4]

To essay such an adventure takes considerable courage, for by abandoning conventional values in favour of the dictates of his inner self he is setting himself apart from the comforts and authority of society in order to follow a lonely road that leads he knows not where. The Hermit illustrates a crisis of will which must be met and overcome by anyone who would advance beyond the common pale.

Conversely, the awareness of conscience is his first glimpse of the Inward Light; the first intimation of the brilliance of the mystic Centre which lies at the end of his quest.

This feeble flickering of the inward light helps guide the Hermit on his way; it is his lantern, by the light of which he can discern a little of the path before him and spy out the obstacles and crevices that lie at his feet.

The stage in life represented by the Hermit has been well described by the philosopher Schopenhauer: "Life may be compared to a piece of embroidery, of which, during the first half of his time, a man gets a sight of the right side, and during the second half, of the wrong. The wrong side is not so pretty as the right, but it is more instructive; it shows the way in which the threads have been worked together."[5]

The figure of the Hermit is also a powerful psychic image who sometimes appears in dreams or visions. He personifies the Wise Old Man, the teacher who points out the thread of meaning that is woven into the apparent chaos of life. He illuminates the primeval darkness with the light of higher consciousness, and drives away the shadows of the night.

The negative aspect of the Hermit shows he whose mind has locked fast in an attitude of stubborn dogmatism, unable to adopt new concepts or shed old ones. He is cloaked in ignorance, and the light of his higher self is shielded from the winds of change which threaten his complacency. The staff upon which he leans is then the body of fixed doctrine which he is unable to discard.

Divinatory meanings:

Upright: Indicates a need to retire from activities in order to think and plan. A warning against attempting headlong progress without careful planning to support it. Help and advice from a wise counsellor—this may be another person, or the voice of one's own inner self. A need to take things slowly, seeking out the right path before proceeding further. Discretion and silence.

Reversed: Refusal to listen to sound advice. Reliance on one's own inadequate resources when help is offered. A turning away from offers of assistance. Obstinate rejection of wisdom. Uncalled-for suspicion of the motives of others. Fear of innovation.

WHEEL of FORTUNE

X THE WHEEL OF FORTUNE

A six-spoked wooden wheel hangs from a twin-pillared frame. Poised on a platform above the wheel sits a strange figure, perhaps a crudely-drawn dragon, winged and crowned and bearing a raised sword. On the right-hand side of the Wheel an equally odd creature—possibly an ass—is clinging as it is drawn upwards. On the left side of the Wheel, descending, is suspended what seems to be an ape. In some Tarot packs a monkey is depicted squatting on the ground, turning the handle which rotates the wheel.

The Wheel of Fortune is card ten in the Tarot sequence. Ten is the first of the double numbers, therefore it symbolises a new beginning and the completion of the earlier series. Traditionally it is thought of as a perfect number, and the symbol of perfection is the circle or wheel.

The second half of the quest has now begun. Examining the inner world of dreams and visions with the light of his intuition,

78

the Hermit observes the strange images that rise before him from the depths. The sinking of his mind beneath the threshold of normal awareness allows unconscious material to rise above the surface.

The wheel is a mandala, a symbol of psychic wholeness and inner order.

The appearance of the Wheel of Fortune here indicates that a major stage on the quest has been reached. The Hermit has cast himself free from the bonds of society, and his sacrifice is rewarded; out of the darkness the unconscious, hidden side of himself rises up to greet him as the wheel turns.

Only by a direct confrontation with the contents of the unconscious can they be brought into the light of day, recognised and comprehended. Only by such understanding can consciousness be illuminated and expanded, and the doubts raised earlier by Justice be satisfied.

The symbol of the wheel brings with it peace of mind, the resolution of guilt, and an affirmation of the fundamental order existing at all levels of the universe.

To the ancient Egyptians the cynocephalus, or dog-headed baboon, was sacred to Thoth, Lord of Magic and the prototype of Hermes, because it was considered the highest of the apes and thus the representative of the forces of the unconscious that transcend the conscious mind.

The dog-like creature descending the wheel can be seen as the "domesticated" self entering the depths, whilst the ascending beast is the "untamed" unconscious emerging into the light of day. The monkey sometimes placed at the base of the wheel might represent the libido or fundamental life-force which is the motive-power of the wheel, whilst the dragon above is the transformed figure of Justice standing ready to repel any whose destiny has not prepared him for the journey into the underworld.

The hub of the wheel is the still mystic Centre, surrounded by the radiating paths that lead to the Self. Although this card does not represent the final goal of the seeker, the centre itself, yet it reveals a stage of development which few attain. The way beyond leads down into the realms of night, the Lunar land where the ego has no authority and must abdicate in favour of powers which it cannot comprehend.

The traditional interpretation of this card says that the beast descending the wheel represents the unevolved soul sinking into the restriction of matter, symbolised by the ape. The ascending creature is the evolving being rising slowly above the material bonds that enslave him.

But above sits the dragon with the sword, ready, when death has finally released him from his body, to thrust him back on to the turning wheel, down into incarnation once more. Finally, through innumerable lives, he reaches the stage at which the physical universe has nothing more to teach him, and he has earned the right to progress to higher spheres. At this point the dragon loses its fearsome aspect, and instead of turning him back on the downward path with the point of its sword, uses the sharp blade to sever his bonds and give him release.

In the mundane world the Wheel of Fortune points to the laws that govern life and death—the principle of change within which nothing is constant, nothing can be grasped and held with certainty. The only freedom from the wheel possible whilst on earth comes through accepting its motion and living in harmony with it.

The negative side of the wheel shows the fate of he who is totally preoccupied with his immediate life and who identifies himself with the changing face of his personality. Unable to stand back and view existence in a wider perspective, he remains ignorant of the lessons it might teach him. Unable to learn from his mistakes, he travels on, sure in his own mind that his troubles are temporary and soon to be solved through his own efforts plus a little luck. He is the constant prey of whatever the Fates have in store for him, and is thus inextricably caught up in the round of births and deaths.

Divinatory meanings:

Upright: The commencement of a new cycle in one's affairs. The processes of destiny, working through time. Events of great moment, over which one can have no personal influence. The operation of the laws of fortune. The solving of a problem through the progression of circumstances. The reaping of what has been sown—generally an auspicious omen.

Reversed: A turn for the worse. Irreversible adversities which can only be endured until the wheel revolves full circle in the fullness of time. The closing of a cycle of fortune.

XI

FORTITUDE

XI Fortitude

A young woman firmly grasps the jaws of a powerful lion that stands before her. On her head is a large and curiously shaped hat, and a voluminous cloak hangs from her shoulders. She seems calm and undisturbed despite her predicament.

Fortitude is the second of the four Virtues to appear in the Tarot pack. The picture of Fortitude as a young woman in the act of restraining a lion is a common Medieval image.

This card is numbered eleven, the second of the double numbers. As it follows immediately after the perfect number ten, eleven is traditionally indicative of vulnerability, danger, and overstepping the mark. Being formed in Arabic numerals from the number one repeated, it is similar to the number two in that it suggests tension, opposition, and a struggle to reconcile divergent qualities.

These possibilities are all apparent in the Tarot card.

The first image which the Hermit encounters on his journey

into the underworld of the unconscious is his own shadow, a distorted reflection of himself. In the shadow live all the darker aspects of his being which his personality has been unable to accept, aspects which up till now have only manifested themselves to him in dark thoughts or troubled dreams.

The conscious mind and its shadow are both parts of a psychic whole, and until the two are reconciled no further development can take place. Most people cannot face the confrontation with the shadow, and its dark qualities are projected on to the world outside. Only a few succeed in breaking through this web of self-delusion to the unnerving truth that the shadow lies within themselves.

In most ancient myths dealing with the quest of the hero, the hero first needs a friend, often a primitive "wild man", who will undertake the adventure with him. The combined talents of the hero and his friend are required to overcome the perils that lie ahead. But first they must do battle together, for only if the hero can subdue the wild man may they proceed together.

Jung has said: "The self is made manifest in the opposites and in the conflict between them; it is a *coincidentia oppositorum*. Hence the way to the self begins with conflict."[6]

This critical encounter is portrayed in the Tarot card Fortitude. We saw in the last card, the Wheel of Fortune, that the studied introversion of the hermit had begun to bring images from the unconscious into his field of awareness. Here, the shadow—symbolised by a lion, alchemical symbol of the forces of instinct—is being firmly subdued by the seeker, who is represented as a young woman to indicate that gentleness rather than severity is the quality needed for success.

The imagery here suggests the Biblical story of Samson slaying the lion, after which a swarm of bees lived in the carcase. In some old Tarot packs Fortitude is indicated by the figure of Samson strangling the lion.

The defeat of the lion represents the reconciliation with instinctive desires, which releases the energies locked up in the shadow, and reunites the conscious mind with the long-lost paths to the inner centre.

In mundane terms Fortitude represents the individual who

through discipline attains self-control, freeing him from the constant distractions and changes of mood to which ordinary men are prey. The young woman, like the charioteer in card VII, represents a type of strength—but the passive, inner strength of steadfast purpose; not the positive, outer strength of action.

In her negative aspect she shows the conscious suppression of instinctive needs, for fear of the potential power to destroy the veneer of civilised convention within which the insecure mind can feel safe.

Divinatory meanings:
Upright: Opportunity to put plans into action if one has the courage to take a risk. Morally, the defeat of base impulses. Reconciliation with an enemy—this can be outside oneself, or else refer to unruly forces within.
Reversed: Defeat, surrender to unworthy impulses, failure of nerve leading to loss of opportunity.

XII

THE HANGED MAN

XII THE HANGED MAN

A young man hangs upside-down in the air, suspended by his right
ankle from a wooden gibbet. His hands appear to be tied behind
his back, and his left leg hangs loosely behind his right. His face
shows an expression of calm detachment, and in some packs his
head is surrounded by a halo.

The Hanged Man is one of the strangest of the Tarot images. It
cannot be found in any orthodox Christian symbology, and is
one of the clearest indications that the Tarot trumps were designed
to illustrate some non-Christian system of belief.

The card is numbered twelve. In Arabic numerals it is a combination of the numbers one and two, signifying the interaction
of unity with duality which gives birth to a third dimension. The
perils of number eleven have been resolved, therefore it is a
symbol of renewal and salvation.

The hero has confronted the raging lion and knows it to be his
very own shadow which wrestles with him. He becomes agonisingly

aware that he is not one person, the conscious self he identifies with, but only part of a greater whole. He sees two halves which are antagonistic to one another, yet are at the same time complementary. He cannot go back and reclaim the assured selfhood of his youth, yet equally he must not submit to his shadow. His only hope is to become free of both opponents, to step back into a central position in which he is balanced between the two.

In so doing, he realises that in casting himself off from the solid ground of his past consciousness, he can only trust that a larger power will support him and stop him falling into a psychic void. In order to proceed he must have the courage to let go of all he has learnt, voluntarily release the grip of intellect, and allow the deeper forces within to take the reins.

To deliberately float oneself on the secret tides of the unconscious implies a deliberate reversal of the teachings and values of the outer world, and the acceptance of a grave risk—the laws and values of the inner worlds are in many cases the exact reverse of those we are familiar with, and are only transgressed at one's peril.

The seeker now has to pass two trials—that of courage, and that of faith. Courage, in that he must sacrifice all that his conscious mind holds dear, and also renounce the instinctual demands of his shadow; faith, in that he must believe in the existence of a higher self which transcends his conscious awareness.

According to Jung: "By descending into the unconscious, the conscious mind puts itself in a perilous position, for it is apparently extinguishing itself."[7]

The Hanged Man illustrates he who has taken his life in his hands and cast himself head first into the depths. His action has not been foolhardy, however, for he hangs safely suspended by the knot of his own faith. The knot is sometimes depicted as being formed from the living branch of a tree: the World Tree, or Tree of Life that grows through every plane of the cosmos. The Hanged Man's enraptured face reveals that his sacrifice has not been in vain, and that he has his reward. His torture is transmuted into ecstasy.

Because he is balanced equally between the demands of both

the conscious mind and its shadow, he finds himself in a blissful state of total freedom from desire.

The hanging of a sacrificial victim from a tree is a well-known feature of religious cults in several parts of the world. In the Icelandic Sagas, which had been written down before the middle of the 13th century, the Norse god Odin described how he hanged himself on the World Ash in order to discover the mystic runes:

> "I know that I hung
> in the windy tree
> for nine full nights.
> Wounded by the spear,
> consecrated to Odin,
> an offering to myself
> on the tree
> whose roots are unknown."[8]

In Sumerian rites the God Attis was hung in effigy each year on a pine tree. The tree is a symbol of the mother as the source of all sustenance; those who die on the tree are therefore being reunited with their source, through which they may be reborn into new life. By sacrificing his life the Hanged Man opens the way to his rebirth into the immortality of the spirit.

The traditional interpretation of this card is that in order to achieve real success and fulfilment one must align oneself with the rules of the universe rather than the laws of man. To do this requires courage, fortitude, and faith in the values of the spirit; but for those who dare to assert their independence in this fashion a reward will come—the gift of serenity and inward peace.

In his negative aspect The Hanged Man is the vague idealist who lives in his own imaginary dream world, located neither in Heaven nor on earth, but suspended somewhere between the two in a place of his own invention. His eyes are turned inward and he is blind to the beauty that lies all around him, as he hangs by the thread of his wild fantasy.

Divinatory meanings:
Upright: The ability to adapt to changing circumstances.

Flexibility of mind. Willingness to submit oneself to the dictates of the inner self and cast aside practical considerations when the time is right. Wisdom and guidance from the unconscious.

Reversed: Over-reliance on the concrete mind. Materialism. A warning of impending psychic disorder through an inability to accept the reality of the unconscious. An inner struggle ending in defeat.

XIII DEATH

An animated human skeleton, armed with a large scythe, is mowing a field of fertile black earth. His crop is not corn but human bodies, bits of which can be seen scattered at his feet. Two decapitated heads, one crowned, are shown; their eyes open and their flesh apparently firm. Behind the skeleton in some packs a river flows from left to right, and near the horizon two pillars or pylons frame the sun which is low in the sky.

The number of this card, thirteen, is emblematic of death, and has unfortunate connotations even today. The appearance of the Grim Reaper beneath this number seems very appropriate. The Arabic number thirteen is made up of the numbers one and three, and is therefore analogous to the number four as a symbol of order and organisation. Death, though apparently the agent of chaos, is in fact the instigator of a new order which follows life.

This card continues the story of the Hanged Man. His sacrifice having been accepted, he is literally no longer the same person.

His old self is now dead, to be replaced in due course by something new and totally different. His viewpoint has changed from being self-centred to being self-transcendent. In his death lies his opportunity for rebirth.

In Jung's words: "The purpose of the descent as universally exemplified in the myth of the hero is to show that only in the region of danger (watery abyss, cavern, forest, island, castle, etc.) can one find the 'treasure hard to attain' (jewel, virgin, life-potion, victory over death)."[9]

The skeleton depicted here, the stylised image of death, is not a forbidding figure but is instead the liberator, whose keen blade releases consciousness from its old bondage.

It used to be believed that the head was the abode of the soul, and the living heads shown lying here indicate that life is not dependent on its physical shell; when the body is removed the soul can receive its life directly from its true source—the fertile ground of the spirit.

The isolated hands and feet that lie on the earth also show no sign of decomposition. One hand is raised firmly up out of the earth and the feet seem planted where they have fallen. They are not the remains of past life, but the seeds of new.

The river sometimes depicted in the background is the Styx, the black water of death which is also the water of life that leads to rebirth. The seeker is buried in the depths of his own being, waiting for the revivifying contact from the unconscious wellsprings of life that will enable him to realise his rebirth into immortality.

The mundane explanation of this card says that death is the principle of nature which sweeeps away old life and clears the ground for the growth of the new. Without death life could hardly have begun, but death is not the end: old life not only makes way for new, but also supplies the material for its structure. The future springs from the rich loam of the past. Nothing is lost and nothing is wasted; only the form changes.

The skeleton itself symbolises the underlying continuance of life. Although the features and appearance of the individual alter as life progresses, the bone structure which supports those features remains unaltered, and supports the flesh of the old man as it did the youth.

The negative aspect of death points to the painful truth that he is no respecter of persons; all fall who stand before him, and none can escape their inevitable end.

Divinatory meanings:

Upright: An unexpected major change in circumstances, which is nevertheless the natural outcome of a prevailing situation. Destruction which is a blessing in disguise, as it clears the way for something better. The removal from one's life of that which is outdated or superfluous in order that one might move forward into the future unhindered.

Reversed: The enforced removal of something which should have been dispensed with voluntarily, but which is now taken. The element of chance—the apparently wilful aspect of destiny which takes without reason.

XIV

TEMPERANCE

XIV Temperance

A winged angelic figure is shown here pouring liquid from a pitcher held in her right hand to one held in her left. In some versions a small flower decorates her brow. She is clearly seen to be standing out of doors under an open sky.

The image of the Virtue of Temperance as a woman pouring water from one vessel to another is, like the image of Fortitude and Justice, a familiar one from Byzantine and Medieval artistic sources.

The word temperance in this context is meant in the old sense of the mixing of ingredients in the right proportion. This card is therefore emblematic of the conjunction of opposites. It is assigned the number fourteen, which in Arabic numerals is made up of the numbers one and four. The combination of unity and the quaternary produces the pentagon, the five-sided figure illustrating organic growth, inspiration, and the reconciliation of several parts in a greater whole.

Having voluntarily sacrificed his old self, challenged the power of his shadow-side and won freedom from both conscious and sub-conscious desires, the seeker has achieved the position of the severed heads, hands and feet shown in the card Death: cut off from all links with his old existence, safely rooted in the ground of the new. But as yet he is quiescent, merely the seed of new life. After casting aside all that he has, retaining nothing, he has at last entered a state of complete passivity. He no longer believes in his ego as a point of reference when evaluating the world, and is unable to make any value judgements.

At this stage the angel of Temperance appears, filling the void that has been prepared in the seeker's consciousness with the water of new life; redressing the balance between consciousness and the unconscious, giving him the advantage of a new, and far truer, centre from which to act.

Until he was prepared to reject both his ego and its shadow, his higher self could only signal its presence from afar; his human personality left no room for it within the confines of consciousness.

The angel is sometimes shown standing with one foot in a pool of water. The pool symbolises the depths of the unconscious, and she is thus shown as bridging the gap between the outer and inner worlds.

In some versions of this card blue irises grow by the pool. These flowers are named after the Greek goddess Iris, whose symbol was the rainbow. The complete symbolism of the rainbow, which also appears in some Tarot cards, is complex and profound. In one sense it is the beautiful spectrum of light caused by the radiance of the hidden centre shining through the shifting mists of the sub-conscious, and revealing itself to the world of consciousness as a brightly-coloured bridge of hope: the bow of promise.

The Angel of Temperance can be seen as a high aspect of the Anima, the feminine archetypal power who live within the seeker's deep unconscious and is the bearer of creative forces from within. She appears here as a mediator between outer consciousness and the inner self.

In one medieval mystical work she is made to speak thus: "I am the flower of the field and the lily of the valleys. I am the mother of fair love and of fear and of knowledge and of holy hope . . . I am the mediator of the elements, making one to agree with another; that which is warm I make cold and the reverse, and that which is dry I make moist and the reverse, and that which is hard I soften ... "[10]

The mundane interpretation of Temperance, also known as the Angel of Time, suggests the flowing of time from the past into the future; the continuity of life and its transference from one bodily existence to another. This can be held to apply to the theory of reincarnation, or to the continuity of consciousness over and above the death and renewal of the cells of the body.

The negative aspect of Temperance makes her a symbol of frustration, the wastage of creative energy that is tossed back and forth by restricting circumstances or repressive mental attitudes. This is the evil of prejudice founded on narrow, constricting rules of life that do not allow adequate expression of the creative forces of nature.

Divinatory meanings:

Upright: Success is possible through the careful control of volatile factors. Indicates a situation in which circumstances and people must be skilfully combined for progress to continue. A harmonious partnership is sometimes revealed.

Reversed: Opposition created by ineptitude. Progress thwarted by clumsy handling of a potentially helpful situation.

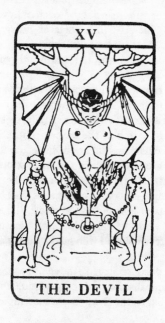

XV THE DEVIL

A conventional figure of the Devil is shown in this card, standing or squatting on a stone plinth. He has a pair of leathery wings and horns grow from his head. His naked body is rather feminine in shape and he has heavy breasts. In some packs he holds a flaming torch in one hand. At his feet stand two lesser demons, also naked, who have horns and tails but no wings. Each demon is restrained by a loose halter round the neck which is fastened by a rope to the Devil's plinth.

This picture of the Devil and his attendants is, like the previous Tarot card, a typical Medieval image. In some old packs he seems to be wearing a helmet with antlers attached, rather than having real horns, and closely resembles the ancient Celtic god Cernunnos who was possibly the prototype of the conventional Christian Devil.

The number of this card is fifteen, made up in Arabic numbers from one and five, which reduces to six. Six is a number of the conjunction of opposite principles (see the Lovers), and is the number of love. The six-pointed star or hexagram is made up of two inter-laced triangles, the upward-pointing alchemical symbol of fire combined with the downward-pointing symbol of water.

Here we have another card concerned with the reconciliation of consciousness with unconscious elements.

Having forged a link with his inner self, the seeker is now able to proceed further in search of the hidden centre. He is no longer isolated inside the narrow confines of his ego but has established contact with the creative forces of the unconscious.

It is at this stage that he first encounters the powerful figures which are not simply part of his personal psyche, but belong to the unconscious strata of humanity as a whole. These are the "primordial images" which belong to the dawn of existence, the cthonic gods whose power is vast and who hold a deadly attraction for the conscious mind.

The collective unconscious, like the ego, has a shadow-side which contains all the unrealised aspects of mankind. In Christianity this is personified as Satan, the Devil, the great tempter, the essence of evil.

In the ancient world this untamed force was embodied in such deities as Dionysus, of whom Jung has said: "Dionysus is the abyss of impassioned dissolution, where all human distinctions are merged in the animal divinity of the primordial psyche—a blissful and terrible experience."[11]

In encountering this figure, the seeker faces a challenge indeed; now he sees why his search is called "the quest of the hero", for only a hero can withstand the power of the Devil. As in the earlier stage of the quest, when he had to confront his own shadow, defeat it, and thus win through to rebirth on a higher level, so here a similar battle must take place.

The meeting with the Devil is the most dangerous encounter of all, because he embodies the energy of the inner self. If he triumphs, then consciousness is flooded with his dark force and the seeker may become a megalomaniac. Re-asserting his ego-centricity, he will be possessed by a sense of his own power and wisdom. He will believe himself to be the recipient of all knowledge, the divinely appointed messenger of God—even the incarnation of God himself. He will be like one possessed as he grasps the attributes of divinity to himself.

But if the challenge of the collective shadow can be met and recognised for what it is, if the power of the Devil can be brought within the sphere of consciousness in a measured and controlled manner, then the forces of darkness may be transformed into the powers of light. In the darkness of death lie the seeds of new life; Satan becomes Lucifer, the shining angel whose name means "The Light-bringer".

The task at this stage of the mystic quest is to comprehend and integrate the deepest urges of nature; urges which follow their own powerful laws and which must be channelled into life-enhancing, evolutionary paths.

In traditional Occult lore the central figure in this card is Pan. In ancient times Pan was one of the gods worshipped as life-giver, the Lord of Fertility, abundance and procreation. The image of Pan is as crucial in its importance as that of Death. Without death, life would be untenable on an over-crowded world; without the life-force, life would never have emerged from the primal swamps.

The lesson of Pan is that nature is not to be despised. Everyone, at whatever stage of development, is embodied in a human frame, equipped with human instincts and emotional drives. But equally, one must not be enslaved by them. The two human figures shown on the card depict this danger—and also show that it can be avoided. The chain that restrains them is not as secure as it might at first appear, and could be removed if they so wished. The powers of instinct exist and are an essential part of life, but they must be subordinated to the civilised aspects of consciousness.

Divinatory meanings:

Upright: Indicates a need to sublimate the lower self, transmuting its energy into usable power. Sometimes shows that hidden forces are at work which must be taken into account when making plans.

Reversed: Lust for power, temptation to abuse one's position for personal ends. Warns of a bid for control by the instinctive side of one's nature. Can also reveal a dangerous repression of the instincts by the intellect.

XVI

THE TOWER

XVI THE TOWER

A sturdy tower, erected on a grassy rise, is struck by lightning. The castellated top of the tower is lifted by the blast and fire strikes deep within. Flames roar from the three windows and a shower of sparks rains down on all sides. Two human figures fall headlong from their stricken refuge.

This card represents the reverse side of the previous one. The opposite of Dionysus, lord of the dark and irrational, is Apollo, god of light and reason; the opposite of Satan, the Devil, is Lucifer, the light-bringer.

The Tower is numbered sixteen in the sequence. Sixteen in Arabic numbers is made up of one and six, which reduce to seven. Seven is a solar number designating power and positive action. In card seven, the Chariot, we saw the influence of the sun in its benign aspect in the person of Helios; here we see the raw power of cosmic energy striking down unshielded.

The lightning-flash was one of the attributes of Jupiter—the bolt of Jove—and also figures prominently in Mahayana and Tantric Buddhism as a symbol of the overpowering light of truth in which all falsehood, and ultimately all duality, is destroyed. It is the flash of inner illumination which brings the freedom of enlightenment.

In French Tarot packs this card is generally entitled *La Maison Dieu*, or House of God. Possibly this is a misreading of the Italian *caso*, meaning chance or fate, as *casa*, meaning house.

The top of the tower is seen to have been struck off by a fiery bolt from Heaven. Symbolically the crown of an edifice frequently represents the peak of consciousness, revealing that in its flashing descent the lightning of pure selfhood, the primal energy of the psyche, strikes aside and rends all structures of the ego.

Having gathered to himself and accepted the true nature of the Devil, the seeker sees him transformed into Lucifer, who embodies the purity of Divine truth. His shattering bolt negates all previous concepts, as did the sacrifice of the Hanged Man at a less profound level.

Human consciousness here is at last in direct contact with the primary forces of the hidden centre, the goal of the mystic quest. The light of Lucifer is not the gentle radiance of intuition filtering up from the depths, but the full glare of God-consciousness, undimmed light such as blinded Paul on the road to Damascus.

An uncanonical saying of Jesus states: "He who is near unto me is near unto the fire."[12] The flux and fire of life are essential to the achievement of wholeness. The alchemists conceived their *aqua nostra* or water of life to be *ignis* (fire). The all-dissolving *aqua nostra* is a basic ingredient in the production of the Stone of the Wise which confers immortality.

The devastating impact of this fire can free the mind from its fetters and open the way that leads to the centre; but if the conscious mind is not prepared, not strongly built on firm foundations, it may end in catastrophe. In psychological terms the outcome will be dissociation, the division of the mind against itself.

The power of the lightning flash can transform the tower of consciousness into "The House of God" or else shatter it irrevocably.

In mundane terms The Tower suggests the destruction of an

out-dated philosophy which is unable to adapt to new conditions. As the human mind develops it easily absorbs new ideas and concepts, using them to build a mental framework which will serve it as a guide during its life. But as the mind matures its principles tend to harden and gradually become fixed, and it becomes unable to accept fresh material which will not fit easil 'nto the existing structure.

Thus it loses contact with the dynamism of reality. Its enclosing walls of dogmatic opinion become unable to adapt to changing circumstances, and if faced with a major challenge of ideas it can only collapse, leaving the bewildered mind within to cope as best it may with the apparent chaos that surrounds it. The lesson here is that any structure is only defensible as long as it remains flexible and capable of evolution; life itself is in a state of constant flux and no merely human construction can hope to survive if it cannot adapt.

Divinatory meanings:

Upright: Suffering of an individual through the forces of destiny being worked out in the world. The apparent unfairness of natural disasters which strike all, just or unjust alike.

Reversed: The calling down of a disaster which might have been avoided. Unnecessary suffering. Self-undoing.

XVII

THE STAR

XVII THE STAR

A naked girl is seen kneeling by the edge of a stream or pool, pouring water from two pitchers. Behind her, in most versions, can be seen a tree with a bird hovering over it. In the sky above eight stars are visible. One star is distinctive in size and shape.

This card is numbered seventeen, which in Arabic numerals reduces to eight. Because of its shape the number eight in Medieval times was considered a symbol of renewal and rebirth, and was therefore linked with baptism. Also, the eighth sphere of the firmament was thought to be that occupied by the fixed stars.

The star shining out of the night is an emblem of the spirit, the mystical Centre, and of the call of destiny. To the alchemist the star was a symbol of the imagination, by which he was linked to the powers of the unconscious and to the material substances that he hoped to transform.

After the storm and lightning of the last card comes the rain which brings with it peace, refreshment and the stirring of new life.

The water which is being poured forth is the *aqua nostra*, the Water of Life or energy of the psyche which is needed to transfer consciousness from the sublunary world to higher spheres.

In the ancient mysteries of Mithras occurred the passage: "I am a star that wanders with you and shines up from the depths."[13]

Having undergone the initiation of fire, the hero now submits to the baptism of water as the flames are quenched by the healing waters of life. The waters pour forth on the earth and into the pool in equal quantities; consciousness and the unconscious are equilibrated and conjoined as psychic conflict is again resolved.

Although the journey is still not at an end, the mystic centre yet to be reached, the presence of the star assures him that his travels are nearing their completion. In the distance can be seen the Tree of Life, an intimation of the immortality that lies ahead, whilst over the crown of the tree hovers the sacred dove, symbol of the Holy Spirit, the divine messenger.

The seeker's faith has been rewarded; after the purifying fire has opened his eyes he need no longer stumble blindly onwards through the night of spiritual darkness, guided only by the flicker of his intellect and the muffled call of his higher self. The presence of the star assures him that his quest has not been in vain, and that in due time the sun will rise and he will stand in the supernal light.

The mundane interpretation of The Star shows the understanding and lack of prejudice which is possible when the doors of the mind stand open. In contrast to the previous image, The Tower, the consciousness symbolised here is not fixed and enclosed within itself, but is open and free like the wide landscape shown in the card.

Thus it is able to receive the influx of original insight, both consciously (the water pouring on the ground), and subconsciously (the water pouring into the pool). The stars shining above represent the higher aspirations which constantly beckon the mind on to fresh heights, keeping at bay the dark shadows of complacency and ignorance. In the negative aspect of this card these possibilities are denied.

Divinatory meanings:

Upright: Insight into possibilities which lie in the future, offering hope and fulfilment. A widening of horizons, physical or mental. New life and vigour appearing as a gift from the gods.

Reversed: Rigidity of mind which cannot expand beyond its familiar boundaries to take in new opportunities for progress. Inability or reluctance to widen one's viewpoint. Self-doubt, lack of trust.

XVIII

THE MOON

XVIII THE MOON

At the foot of this card lies a deep, mysterious pool, out of which a crayfish is attempting to crawl on to the dry land. A path leads up from the pool and wends its way to the horizon. It is guarded by two animals—in some packs these are both dogs, in others a dog and a wolf. Further in the distance can be seen a pair of forbidding towers which form a gateway to the mysterious regions beyond. Above, a full moon hangs in the night sky. Drops of moisture float suspended in the air as if drawn upwards by the power of the moon.

The symbolism of the Moon suggests the beliefs of the heretical Cathari, who taught that after death the souls of the perfect are drawn up to celestial bliss whilst lesser men are reincarnated in animal form.

It is numbered eighteen in the sequence, which in Arabic numerals reduces to nine. Being the last of the single numbers it reveals that this card represents the final part of another stage of the quest, and like card number nine, the Hermit, it is an image of solitude and vulnerability.

The Star has shown the hero that the end is almost in sight, but now he must journey towards the dawn along a path which is badly lit and hard to discern. His human faculties have reached their uttermost limit; he must discard all the senses which have guided him this far and offer himself completely to the utterly non-rational influence of the inward light.

If he has the courage to follow it will lead him along the path that gives entrance into the secret realm of the higher self.

Anciently, the Moon was often believed to be the abode of the dead. The souls of the dying would leave their bodies and be drawn silently up into the Moon, where they would be kept safe until the time of rebirth. Similarly, the Moon symbolised the maternal womb which was the giver forth of new life. Thus the Moon had a dual aspect; it was feared as the dark cavern of death, and revered as the portal into new life.

Its negative aspect was symbolised by Hecate, guardian of the gates of Hades, one of whose main attributes was the dog. Hecate was the dark mother who brought lunacy to those who defied her, yet whose challenge must be met if the "treasure hard to attain", new life, was to be won.

The dark realm of Hecate is illustrated here. At the foot of the card is a crayfish, symbol of the primitive devouring forces of the unconscious which have to be overcome. In the middle distance are the wolf and the dog, guides to the land of the dead, who are also unstable and not to be trusted. Behind them are the pylons of the gateway into Hades, the portal of the dark womb, whilst above all hangs the moon itself, drawing souls to it with its irresistible magic power.

The hero is at a critical stage where his existence lies in the balance. If he allows himself to be entranced by the glamour of the moon his quest is at an end. His life will be drained from him until he is only an empty shell.

But if he forces himself onwards, not straying from the narrow path that lies before him and not allowing himself to be deceived by the spells of illusion cast around him, he will win through to the further side of the dismal cavern and emerge to the light of a new day.

The negative meaning of this card gives a warning against the dangers of uncontrolled imagination, when fantasy is indulged in as a means of escape from the world of reality. In this way consciousness is laid open to invasion from the unintegrated and destructive forces of the unconscious.

Divinatory meanings:

Upright: A crisis of faith—only intuition, not reason, can carry the querent forward. A situation in which one has only oneself to rely on.

Reversed: Failure of nerve. Fear of stepping beyond safe boundaries. A choice of what is, in preference to what might be.

XIX **T**HE **S**UN

Two children are shown here standing, or dancing, before a wall.
In some packs they are seen to be enclosed within a fairy ring, and
luxuriant sunflowers grow over the wall behind them. The sun
hangs in the sky above, and drops of liquid fall from its rays.

The Sun is numbered nineteen in the sequence, which in
Arabic numerals reduces to ten. Ten symbolises a return to unity
out of multiplicity, and indicates attainment. Like card number
ten, the Wheel of Fortune, the Sun suggests the protective qualities
of the mandala and through it an approach to the mystic Centre.

The realm of the collective psyche is often represented poetically
as the "children's land", the country of innocence and undifferentiated consciousness, echoing the words of Jesus: "Unless ye
be converted, and become as little children, ye shall not enter into
the kingdom of heaven."[14]

The children depicted on this Tarot card are shown to be within
an enclosed space, a *temenos* or magic circle which acts as a shield

protecting them from the perils of the soul, a place of refuge in which they can rest and grow.

The hero has successfully withstood the allure of the lunar night and has won through to the sunlit garden beyond. He has traversed the land of the dead and emerged into new life. In this card his twin halves are seen as children, re-united beneath the benign sun of the spirit; the pure and unclouded light of the inner self. They are dancing for joy within the Hidden Garden of the Soul.

His old self is dead and he no longer sees with the eyes of a mortal; his new life unfolds beneath the regenerative rays of the central sun and he gazes out with the innocence of a new-born child. Consciousness has triumphed over the deadly perils of the unconscious and is delivered from the underworld of Hecate. The river of death has led the way to the fountain of youth.

But even now the quest is not quite at an end. The sun is still floating away out of reach, and though the twins are united in their dance they are still separated from one another and from the sun which is the one true centre and the mystic goal.

Before the final step can be taken the opposites must unite and thus transcend their duality. Only in this way can the hero's immortality be assured. The rather benign appearance of the sun in this card belies its immeasurable strength. The reborn personality could not yet withstand its raw power. The wall behind the children symbolises the veil which remains drawn before its burning rays. Its life-enhancing properties are shown by the sunflowers that hang over the wall, and by the falling drops of dew.

Until the children attain their full stature they cannot proceed further. They are like embryos in the womb which must mature before they can be born.

The sun is a symbol of psychic wholeness, the undivided communion of consciousness and the unconscious. The twin halves of the psyche are represented as children because they are still a step away from full integration; still in need of protection from the full heat of the sun.

The negative mundane aspect of this card can be said to represent those who spend their lives "playing in the sun", who are absorbed in the pursuit of physical happiness and who remain oblivious to the world that lies outside their personal pleasure-garden. They are as inncocent, as unthinking, and as potentially cruel as children.

Divinatory meanings:

Upright: Vindication of daring ideas, success and achievement against all odds. The triumph of the innovator, the man of imagination. The gaining of a safe refuge after a period of peril. Acclaim, approval, a just reward.

Reversed: Misjudgement which ends in failure and ignomy. The exposure of one who has succeeded by doubtful means. Fantasies of success replacing real attainment.

XX

JUDGEMENT

XX JUDGEMENT

A winged angel appears in the sky blowing a trumpet. As if in response, three naked figures rise up from the earth beneath. In some packs two of the figures are emerging from the sea, whilst the third, central figure stands in a tomb.

This card depicts the familiar scene of the Last Judgement, when an archangel shall blow the last trump and the dead shall rise from their graves. The card is number twenty in the sequence, which symbolises the duality of number two on a higher plane. Here again we see the opposition of the higher and the lower, but now they are drawing closer together and proceeding towards a final synthesis.

The three figures depicted here are the divine brother-sister pair of the last card, now grown to adulthood, with between them the child of their union. The period of patient growth symbolised by the Sun is now at an end. The angel of resurrection blows his mighty horn and the psyche is released from the walls that imprison it. Its two halves are now mature; they have reached their full potential and between them stands the Divine Child, or regenerated self.

In psychology the dream or vision of the Divine Child heralds some major stage in spiritual development; to the alchemists he was a symbol of the Philosopher's Stone, the treasure hard to attain; as the youthful "God within" he is the ultimate guide to the mystic centre, the goal of the heroic quest.

The trumpet-call, the summons from the Eternal, announces that the arduous search is about to reach its fulfilment. The individual elements of the psyche have reached full integration and are being reborn. The last shadow of illusion is about to melt away, bringing the Great Work to its consummation.

The angel's banner, a scarlet cross on a white ground, symbolises the meeting place of all opposites. It is the great conjunction, the still heart of the Wheel of Fortune which has now ceased its motion; the timeless hub of the cosmos.

The sea from which the figures are emerging is situated midway between earth and sky, signifying the transitional stage between life and death, or death and rebirth. It is the inland sea, the waters of the womb wherein new life develops within a protected and enclosed environment—thus echoing the symbolism of the previous card: the walled Garden of Eden.

In the outer world this card refers to the creative impulse in man which calls forth the highest within him; the strains of divine discontent that keep him striving upwards to new heights of endeavour.

The negative aspect of Judgement implies not that the trumpet-call will not be heard, but that it will be misinterpreted; leading to either a search for lost youth, or that "yearning after strange gods" which causes many Western seekers to study Eastern systems of attainment for which they are fundamentally unsuited.

Divinatory meanings:

Upright: Joy in accomplishment. A new lease of life. A return to health. Justified pleasure in achievement.

Reversed: Loss, guilt, reproach for wasted opportunities. Punishment for failure.

XXI

THE WORLD

XXI THE WORLD

A youthful figure dances in the midst of an encircling wreath. Her only clothing is a loose veil, and in each hand she carries a wand. Surrounding the wreath are the four tetramorphs, the angel, eagle, lion and bull, emblems of the evangelists in Christian iconography.

The figure seen here represents the goal of the alchemists, the *Anima Mundi* freed from the bonds of matter. The conclusion of the Great Work is symbolised by the cosmic egg within which all chaos is reduced to order—the encircling wreath, symbol of ultimate victory. The four mythical beasts stationed in the corners of the card are ancient emblems of protection, the quaternary of powers which ensure the stability of the cosmic processes.

This, the final card in the sequence, is numbered twenty-one. In Arabic numbers this reduces to three, the number of synthesis and creation.

Traditionally the floating veil is said to hide the fact that the dancer is hermaphroditic, combining the physical features of both sexes. This would fit in well with the symbolism of this card as the last stage in the Tarot cycle.

The search is ended, the goal has been reached. The self has at last reached true unity and is indivisible. The contrasexual elements have been reconciled; the psyche no longer holds any illusions concerning its own separateness and is aware that it is conterminous with the entire universe. Poised at the mystic Centre, the androgyne moves with joyful abandon, joining ecstatically in the Dance of Life.

The two wands represent the positive and negative poles of energy between which the tides of the universe flow. They no longer hold the self in their thrall, but are themselves held, almost casually, in the hand. The dancer is seen at the still point where past and future, evolution and involution, action and inaction all intersect and interact.

This Tarot image is a mandala, a prime symbol of psychic wholeness. Such figures generally take the form of a circle, often with a quadratic structure, with some symbol of the self occupying the centre.

Here the hermaphroditic dancer is the self-symbol; the surrounding wreath is the cosmic egg within which the universe is contained; the four figures outside the wreath are the four functions of consciousness, or the four aspects of the self.

Here is a visual guide to the integrated heart of the psyche, the nucleus of primordial energy. It is the squared circle, the diamond lotus, the golden flower, the mystic rose.

According to Jung: "In alchemy the egg stands for the chaos apprehended by the artifex, the *prima materia* containing the captive world-soul. Out of the egg—symbolised by the round cooking-vessel—will rise the eagle or phoenix, the liberated soul, which is ultimately identical with the Anthropos who was imprisoned in the embrace of Physis."[15]

Viewed in terms of the whole Tarot sequence, The World can be seen both as the culmination of the quest, and also as containing the seeds of fresh endeavour on higher planes. If the encircling wreath is viewed as the uterus, and the enclosed being as the undifferentiated embryo growing within, then it leads naturally on to the next card, The Fool, symbol of the newly born child commencing its life's journey. And so the Ring of Return revolves once more.

Divinatory meanings:

Upright: The final and successful completion of any matter in hand. The summing-up of a question or series of circumstances. A culmination of events. The ending of a cycle of destiny.

Reversed: Stagnation, loss of momentum, failure of will, fixity and the circling of energy in established and outmoded channels.

THE FOOL

THE FOOL

When he appears at the end of the sequence the Fool has completed his journey, and he passes gaily through the world, the appearance of which has been transformed by his own inner transformation. Where once was discord, all is now harmony; where despair held sway, fulfilment now reigns; where drab ugliness crowded in on every side, every detail of the universe is now radiant with meaningful beauty.

The fool ignores the precipice beneath his feet because he knows that he is immortal and cannot be harmed. He no longer identifies himself with his physical body or with his earthly personality, and therefore does not fear for his safety. The dog biting at his thigh, which represents the outmoded thoughts and values of mundane existence, is likewise ignored as he proceeds along his way.

The sun above is the pure light of the spirit shining down on him, and the white roses that grow at his heels symbolise the fruits of the spirit springing up in his footsteps.

He does not travel empty-handed, for he carries with him his accumulated store of supernal wisdom—contained in his satchel which sometimes appears embroidered with an eye, signifying spiritual knowledge—and also the complete psychic integration which is the prize of his past struggles, symbolised by the white rose he carries in his hand.

The butterfly which engages his attention embodies the Spirit of Life, still leading him on to new adventures and even higher attainment.

5

THE ESOTERIC TAROT

INTEREST IN TAROT cards as anything more than an amusing game or method of fortune-telling lay dormant until the late 18th century, when they were taken up by a French writer, Antoine Court de Gébelin (1725–1784). Gébelin was an amateur scholar whose interests embraced mathematics, natural history, languages, mythology and the relics of antiquity.

Between the years 1773 and 1784 he published nine volumes of a massive work entitled *Le Monde Primitif Analyse et Compare avec le Monde Moderne*, which was uncompleted at the time of his death. It has been described as "a work of disproportionate erudition, on a plan too vast for the labours of a single individual" but it remains an impressive monument to a remarkable man.

The eighth volume of *Le Monde Primitif*, which was published in Paris in 1781, included a section entitled *Le Jeu des Tarots*.[1] In it Gébelin said: "If one were to know that in our days there existed a work of ancient Egypt, one of their books that escaped malicious destruction . . . a book about their most pure and interesting doctrines, everybody would be eager no doubt to know such an extraordinary and precious work." This "book" was the pack of Tarot cards.

He had become interested in the Tarot after being shown a pack at a friend's house in Paris, and upon learning that these cards were known throughout a large part of Europe he decided to trace their origin.

At this time the mysterious land of Egypt was receiving much learned attention, but as no key to deciphering hieroglyphics had been found, scholars had to rely solely on the reports of ancient authors such as Herodotus, Iamblichus and Plutarch when trying to reconstruct a picture of Egyptian life and thought.

Gébelin surmised that the pack of Tarot cards was the remnant of an Egyptian book of learning—the Book of Thoth, Lord of Magic. He asserted that within the symbolism of the Tarot images were to be found the keys to the wisdom and occult powers of the ancient world.

In 1799, only eighteen years after the publication of *Le Jeu des Tarots*, one of Napoleon's officers stationed in Egypt discovered at the town of Rosetta a fragment of basalt bearing a dual inscription in Greek and hieroglyphics. The finding of the Rosetta Stone led to the gradual decipherment of Egyptian writing, which enabled archeologists to build up an accurate picture of life in ancient Egypt—a picture which did not include the Tarot cards or anything which resembled them in symbolism.

But by this time Gébelin's romantic theory had gained popular approval and the support of other, less discriminating writers. First in the field was a Parisian barber and wig-maker called Alliette, whose first pronouncements on the subject of the Tarot appeared in 1783, only two years after the publication of the final volume of *Le Monde Primitif*.

Under the pen-name Etteilla (his own name spelt backwards) he published several books between the years 1783 and 1787,[2] and more than one Tarot pack based on his own innovations—which he claimed were restorations of the original Egyptian designs that had become corrupt and distorted through the centuries.

Etteilla and his occult teachings were popular in France for many years, and the *Tarots d'Etteilla* are still being produced today.[3] He claimed to have studied the mysteries of the cards for more than thirty years, and his emphasis on their use in divination was possibly the direct cause of the resurgence of interest in all forms of prognostication which occurred in Napoleonic France.

Marie Lenormand (1772–1843),[4] who is said to have predicted the marriage of Napoleon I to Josephine, employed a species of Tarot cards—though very much altered—in her work. She attained a position of some influence, being consulted by eminent clients such as Czar Alexander I of Russia, and was known as "La Sibylle du Faubourg Saint-Germain" after her place of residence.

After the time of Etteilla several uncommitted scholars who were interested in the general origin of playing cards commented on the Tarot pack. In England Samuel Weller Singer repeated in his book published in 1816[5] the earlier theory of Covelluzo that the cards were Arabian and first entered Europe through Italy.

In 1848 W. A. Chatto published a serious and comprehensive account of playing cards,[6] giving an account of their history, manufacture, symbolism and use in games. In an interesting section devoted to Tarot cards he concluded that they were probably the original European playing cards but that too little was known for certain about them to ascertain their origin.

In 1854 the French writer P. Boiteau d'Ambly expounded in his book on playing cards[7] the theory that they had originated with the Gypsies, who in his view had come from India. He did not offer much in the way of facts to support this theory.

However, the sober reflections of serious students could not prevail against the romantic fancies of the "Egyptian" school, which had been so enthusiastically broadcast by Etteilla.

The next author to comment on Tarot cards achieved a far greater fame than any of his predecessors, and can be said to have been the originator of the entire modern occult approach to the subject. His name was Alphonse Louis Constant, who called himself Eliphas Lévi Zahed—his own name translated into Hebrew—and wrote under the pen-name Eliphas Lévi. Although he was born of poor parents in 1810, his high intelligence enabled him to obtain a free education at a Catholic seminary. He was ordained a deacon in 1835, but did not carry his ecclesiastical career any further. In 1844 he married a sixteen-year-old girl, and apparently began to take a serious interest in occultism around this time, studying the works of Postel, Ramon Lull, and Cornelius Agrippa.

After some years his wife left him, and by the early 1850's he had attained a wide reputation as an expert in the occult. In 1854 he visited London on the strength of it, hoping to earn money by teaching, but because of his ignorance of English nothing much came of this. In 1855 he published at Paris his first occult work *Dogme de la Haute Magie*, followed in 1856 by a sequel, *Rituel de la Haute Magie*.

Both of these books contained twenty-two chapters, each chapter being an exposition of aspects of magic which were, in Lévi's view, connected symbolically with one of the twenty-two Tarot trumps.

He went on to produce other books, including his ambitious

Histoire de Magie, and made his living for the next twenty years by giving lessons in occultism to eager students.[8]

Although Lévi never produced a book devoted solely to the Tarot cards, his interpretations of them had an immense influence on occultists who followed in his footsteps.

His most important teaching regarding the Tarot was that the cards were closely linked to the esoteric system of the Qabalah; the twenty-two major trumps were allied to the twenty-two letters of the Hebrew alphabet, and the four suits of the Tarot lesser arcana to the four Elements and the four letters of the Divine Name יהוה (Yod, Heh, Vau, Heh or Yahveh).

The Tarot therefore assumed a position of central importance in Lévi's system; in *Rituel de la Haute Magie* he claimed: "The universal key of magical works is that of all ancient religious dogmas—the key of the Kabalah and the Bible, the Little Key of Solomon. Now, this Clavicle, regarded as lost for centuries, has been recovered by us, and we have been able to open the sepulchres of the ancient world, to make the dead speak, to behold the monuments of the past in all their splendour, to understand the enigmas of every sphinx and to penetrate all sanctuaries. Among the ancients the use of this key was permitted to none but the high priests, and even so its secret was confided only to the flower of initiates."[9]

Later in his career Lévi came to believe that the Tarot had been introduced into Europe by the Gypsies, after he had come into contact with the researches of J. A. Vaillant,[10] an early student of gypsy lore.

Lévi never got around to designing a full pack of Tarot cards according to his own ideas, but a pack was later produced by Oswald Wirth which followed these very closely. Wirth was a pupil of the prominent French occultist Stanislas de Guaïta (1860–1897), whose two-volume work *Le Serpent de la Genêse*[11] was based on Tarot symbolism.

Lévi's ideas were also taken up by Dr. Gerard Encausse (1865–1916), who under the pen-name Papus published *Le Tarot des Bohemians* in 1889. This work incorporated Wirth's cards and Lévi's attributions, set against a background of Qabalistic numerology.

Encausse was Spanish by birth, but went to France as a child and graduated from medical school in Paris. He became widely known as a writer on occult subjects[12] and founded an influential school known as *L'Ordre des Silencieux Inconnus*. He also became leader of the *Kabalistic Order of the Rose-Croix* which had been founded by Stanislas de Guaïta in 1888.

Like Lévi, Encausse had a very high opinion of the Tarot, and wrote in *Le Tarot des Bohémians*: "The game of cards called the Tarot, which the Gypsies possess, is the Bible of Bibles. It is the book of Thoth Hermes Trismegistus, the book of Adam, the book of the primitive Revelation of ancient civilisations."[13]

He followed Lévi's attributions of the Tarot trumps to the Hebrew alphabet, as given below. All the cards follow their natural sequence, except The Fool, the unnumbered card, which is placed between card XX, Judgement, and card XXII, The World.

This was because Lévi attributed The Fool to the Hebrew letter Shin, said to symbolise the fire of the spirit, and Shin is the twenty-first letter of the Hebrew alphabet.

ELIPHAS LÉVI'S ATTRIBUTION OF THE TAROT TRUMPS TO THE HEBREW ALPHABET

I	The Magician	א	(Aleph)
II	The High Priestess	ב	(Beth)
III	The Empress	ג	(Gimel)
IV	The Emperor	ד	(Daleth)
V	The High Priest	ה	(Heh)
VI	The Lovers	ו	(Vau)
VII	The Chariot	ז	(Zain)
VIII	Justice	ח	(Cheth)
IX	The Hermit	ט	(Teth)
X	The Wheel of Fortune	י	(Yod)
XI	Fortitude	כ	(Kaph)
XII	The Hanged Man	ל	(Lamed)
XIII	Death	מ	(Mem)
XIV	Temperance	נ	(Nun)

XV The Devil	ס	(Samekh)
XVI The Tower	ע	(Ayin)
XVII The Star	פ	(Peh)
XVIII The Moon	צ	(Tzaddi)
XIX The Sun	ק	(Qoph)
XX Judgement	ר	(Resh)
The Fool	ש	(Shin)
XXII The World	ת	(Tau)

It can fairly be claimed that the work of Lévi and Papus formed the basis of the mainstream of subsequent esoteric development on the continent of Europe. In Britain and America, however, a different influence made itself felt.

This was the Hermetic Order of the Golden Dawn, founded in London *c.* 1887 by three members of an English Masonic body, the *Societas Rosicruciana in Anglia*, which was only open to Master Masons.

The history of the Golden Dawn has been related in detail elsewhere,[14] so suffice it to say that its founders—the Rev. A. F. A. Woodford, Dr. Woodman, and Dr. Wynn Westcott, a London coroner—enlisted the help of a Scottish Freemason called Samuel Liddell Mathers in preparing their Order papers and constructing esoteric initiation rituals.

Mathers, who called himself MacGregor Mathers (and later, when he lived in Paris, Le Comte de Glenstrae), was the guiding light behind the Golden Dawn, and the Order's method of attributing the Tarot cards to the Qabalistic Tree of Life probably originated with him.

The Golden Dawn system of assigning the Tarot major trump cards differs almost completely from that of Lévi and Papus, simply because the unnumbered card, The Fool, was moved to the head of the list, corresponding to the letter Aleph. Thus every card moves down one step, except the final card, the World, which still corresponds to the letter Tau.

The Golden Dawn also linked the twenty-two cards with the elements, signs of the zodiac, and planets. In doing this, Mathers was following the lead of Eliphas Lévi, who had written: "The absolute hieroglyphic science has for its basis an alphabet of which all the gods are letters, and all the letters ideas, all the ideas numbers, and all the numbers perfect signs."[15]

The ambitious aim of the leaders of the Golden Dawn was to combine the knowledge and practices of every occult tradition into one vast all encompassing system of esoteric thought.

The Order teaching was build around the philosophy of the Qabalah, the Jewish mystical system which first became known in Spain in the 12th century. This system differentiates between the totally unknowable Godhead and the God of religious experience, who is an emanation of the Divine Source.

The Qabalists divide this Divine manifestation into ten stages or aspects, called *Sephiroth*. These are formally arranged in a pattern linked together by twenty-two channels or "paths". This diagram is thought of as an anatomy of the Deity, whose garment is the universe. It is known as the Tree of Life.

The ten Sephiroth are arranged in three vertical lines, or columns; the left-hand column is feminine, the right-hand column masculine, whilst the central column reconciles and equilibrates the other two.

If you look at the illustration of the Tree of Life (opposite) you will first see right at the top the words *Ain Soph Aour*. This means "Infinite Light", and refers to the ground of creation, the Godhead, both the source of life and its goal.

Immediately below is the first Sephorah, *Kether*, meaning "The Crown". This is the least tangible form of manifestation, equivalent in the Golden Dawn scheme to the centre of human consciousness, the spirit.

Below are two parallel Sephiroth—*Chokmah*, meaning "Wisdom", and *Binah*, "Understanding". These two form the fundamental polarity of all existence—masculine and feminine, light and dark, positive and negative.

These three initial Sephiroth are known as the three Supernals, which lie far above and beyond the realms of the seven spheres that hang suspended beneath them on the Tree. Between them they give rise to the manifestations of divinity which are apprehended by the human mind.

The next three Sephiroth form an inverted triangle "reflected" beneath the Supernals.

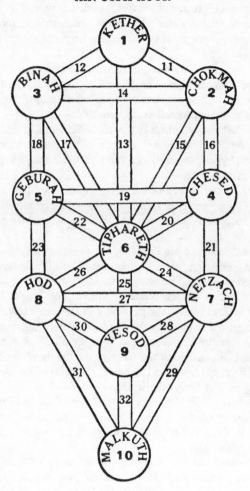

The Tree of Life

Chesed, meaning "Grace", or "Mercy", and *Geburah*, "Power" or "Severity" encompass the powers governing the expansion and construction of forms, and the forces of destruction.

Tiphareth, "Beauty" or "Harmony" balances and reconciles these opposing spheres. It symbolises the height of normal human consciousness.

Below *Tiphareth* is a second "reflected" triangle, commencing with the parallel Sephiroth *Netzach*, "Victory", and *Hod*, "Splendour". These represent, among other things, the human emotions and human intellect respectively.

Suspended beneath them is the ninth Sephirah, *Yesod*, "The Foundation". This is the web of inter-atomic energy which supports the physical universe, and also symbolises the subconscious mind of man.

Finally, at the bottom of the Tree, which is seen to have its roots in Heaven and to grow down towards the Earth, is *Malkuth*, "The Kingdom". This is the visible world, and man's physical body.

The ten Sephiroth are linked by the twenty-two Paths which, to avoid confusion with the numbering of the spheres, are numbered down the Tree from 11 to 32.

Interpreted by modern Western Qabalists, the Tree of Life indicates the way in which the physical world of man is linked to the ultimate ground of being by the stages of Divine emanation. Also, since the Tree of Life shows how the multiplicity of manifested existence is derived from the unity of the Godhead, so, read in reverse, it reveals how man can ascend the paths of the Tree and, in the fullness of time, experience union with God.

The whole magical teaching of the Order of the Golden Dawn was aimed at effecting such a "rising on the planes", and the imagery of the Tarot cards was considered a powerful weapon in the initiate's armoury.

The twenty-two letters of the Hebrew alphabet were always traditionally linked with the twenty-two paths which joined the ten Sephiroth of the Tree of Life. Taking this a stage further, the leaders of the Golden Dawn assigned the twenty-two major Tarot trumps to the paths as well.

They believed that by meditating on the Tarot symbols it is

possible to raise one's consciousness up through the ascending levels of the Tree, experiencing and absorbing the powers of each Sphere as it is encountered, thus achieving an ever increasing degree of spiritual attainment.

To assist the aspiring adept in his inward journey, an elaborate system of correspondences was built up which were intended as signposts to keep him on the right path. For example, the 26th path, linking the Sephirah *Hod* to the Sephirah *Tiphereth* is assigned the Tarot card The Devil, plus such symbols as the zodiacal sign of Capricorn, the odours of musk and civet, the gods Pan, Bacchus and Set, the goat and the ass, and the thistle.

If the initiate exploring the 26th path found himself visualising images such as the element Water, the gods Poseidon or Neptune, the Tarot card The Hanged Man, or the odour of Myrrh, he would know that he had gone astray, because these are all attributes of the 23rd path, linking *Hod* with the Sephirah *Geburah*.

This method of linking the Tarot with a wide system of other images was the cause of a major innovation made in the numbering of the cards at this time. Twelve of the cards were linked with signs of the zodiac which seemed to be symbolically compatible with them. In this way card VIII Justice, was linked with the sign Libra, the Balance, as the card depicts a woman holding a pair of scales; card XI Fortitude, was linked with the sign Leo, because it shows a woman grasping a lion.

But astrologically, Leo precedes Libra in the zodiac, therefore it was decided that the two Tarot cards, Justice and Fortitude, had somehow been counterchanged at some point during their long history. The leaders of the Golden Dawn replaced the cards in what they considered their original, and rightful, place. Fortitude became card VIII, and Justice card XI. This change in numeration has been followed in most of the "esoteric" packs produced subsequently.

MAGICAL CORRESPONDENCES OF THE TAROT TRUMPS ON THE PATHS OF THE TREE OF LIFE ACCORDING TO THE ORDER OF THE GOLDEN DAWN

Tarot trump	Hebrew letter		Path	Astrological attribute
The Fool	א	(Aleph)	11	Air
I The Magician	ב	(Beth)	12	Mercury
II The Papess	ג	(Gimel)	13	Moon
III The Empress	ד	(Daleth)	14	Venus
IV The Emperor	ה	(Heh)	15	Aries
V The Pope	ו	(Vau)	16	Taurus
VI The Lovers	ז	(Zain)	17	Gemini
VII The Chariot	ח	(Cheth)	18	Cancer
VIII Fortitude	ט	(Teth)	19	Leo
IX The Hermit	י	(Yod)	20	Virgo
X The Wheel of Fortune	כ	(Kaph)	21	Jupiter
XI Justice	ל	(Lamed)	22	Libra
XII The Hanged Man	מ	(Mem)	23	Water
XIII Death	נ	(Nun)	24	Scorpio
XIV Temperance	ס	(Samekh)	25	Sagittarius
XV The Devil	ע	(Ayin)	26	Capricorn
XVI The Tower	פ	(Peh)	27	Mars
XVII The Star	צ	(Tzaddi)	28	Aquarius
XVIII The Moon	ק	(Qoph)	29	Pisces
XIX The Sun	ר	(Resh)	30	Sun
XX Judgement	ש	(Shin)	31	Fire
XXI The World	ת	(Tau)	32	Saturn

The Golden Dawn leaders themselves created a pack for the use of their followers, and each of the major trumps was given a title which reflected its significance on the Tree of Life. This pack has never been issued publicly, but a good idea of the Qabalistic Tarot can be gained from the "rectified" Tarot pack published by the

Eight major trump cards from a fortune-telling pack designed and published by Etteilla in the early 19th century. These cards differ very much from the original patterns. Their numerical sequence has been altered and much of the symbolism destroyed. (British Museum: Schreiber collection.)

ETTEILLA

REPOS · REPOS

LA PRESTIGIENSE

LA TEMPÉRANCE

LA TEMPÉRANCE · LA TEMPÉRANCE

LE PRÊTRE

MARIAGE.

LE GRAND PRÊTRE · LE GRAND PRÊTRE

UNION.

FORCE MAJEURE

LE DIABLE · LE DIABLE

FORCE MINEURE

MALADIE.

LE MAGICIEN OU LE BATELEUR · LE MAGICIEN OU LE BATELEUR

MALADIE.

LE JUGEMENT.

LE JUGEMENT DERNIER · LE JUGEMENT DERNIER

LE JUGEMENT.

TRAITRE.

LE CAPUCIN · LE CAPUCIN

FAUX DÉVOT.

FORTUNE.

LA ROUE DE FORTUNE · LA ROUE DE FORTUNE

AUGMENTATION.

XIV

LA TEMPERAN.

XV

IL DIAVOLO

XVI

LA TORRE

XVII

LE STELLE

XVIII

LA·LUNA

XIX

IL SOLE

occult scholar A. E. Waite in 1910. This pack, sometimes known as the Rider pack after the name of its original publishers, is still available today.

Extensive changes can be seen to have been made to some of the original Tarot designs to make them reflect the Qabalistic scheme more closely. In particular, pictorial imagery was carried right through the entire pack. The forty numbered cards of the lesser arcana, which traditionally depict simple formal arrangements of the suit appropriate to each card, in the Waite pack show elaborate scenes.

Waite himself, in a book written to accompany his pack,[16] claimed that these were only meant to illustrate the divinatory meanings of each card, and that no higher significance should be read into them.

But Waite was a member of the Order of the Golden Dawn at this time and obviously incorporated esoteric symbolism into many of his designs. The Golden Dawn leaders had included the entire Tarot pack of seventy-eight cards in their Qabalistic scheme. As well as assigning the twenty-two major trumps to the paths of the Tree of Life, they had applied the forty small cards and the sixteen court cards to the Tree as well. This will be discussed in the following chapters.

Many other Tarot packs have been published in this century, each one reflecting the beliefs of one particular occult group, and many books have been written to elucidate the mysteries of the esoteric Tarot. Others members of the Golden Dawn, as well as Waite, wrote such books, notably Paul Foster Case (1929),[17] Israel Regardie (1932),[18] and Aleister Crowley (1944).[19]

In 1929, an American author, Manly Palmer Hall, issued a Tarot pack drawn by J. A. Knapp, based on Oswald Wirth's

---

Six major trump cards from a pack produced by Gumppenberg in Milan c.1820. These designs were engraved by C. Della Rocca, and reveal how the original symbols were gradually altered by later interpreters. The Devil, for example, has lost his two devotees and his horned helmet; the crayfish crawling from a pool in The Moon has become a lobster on a dish; the two naked children in The Sun are now two elegantly-dressed adults dancing in a formal garden. (British Museum: Schreiber collection.)

ideas, and in 1930 J. A. Knapp published his own pack with a commentary by Manly Palmer Hall. The American *Brotherhood of Light* published an "Egyptian" Tarot, depicting figures crudely derived from ancient Egyptian art, whilst in England the Insight Institute issued a pack said to be based on traditional 15th century designs.

One of the most original—and bizarre—works produced in recent times on the subject of the Tarot cards is *The Book of Thoth* by Aleister Crowley (1875–1947).

Crowley had joined the Golden Dawn in 1898, but later quarrelled with Mathers and founded his own Order, the *Argenteum Astrum*, or Silver Star, in 1905. He saw himself as the voice of a new aeon, the Age of Horus, which was about to supersede the age of Christianity.

The Book of Thoth was printed privately in London in 1944, and has recently been reissued publicly in America. It is based on the Golden Dawn Tarot attributions, altered to fit Crowley's personal philosophy. The book is illustrated with a pack designed under his direction by Lady Freida Harris. Artistically this is probably the most accomplished esoteric pack, but as Crowley's extreme ideas have in the main been rejected or ignored by other occultists, it has not proved influential.

Only one of his many innovations has been widely accepted. This involves the attribution of the Tarot trumps to the Hebrew alphabet and the Tree of Life. Crowley came to the conclusion that for the Tarot to "fit" the scheme of the Tree perfectly, two more cards needed to be counterchanged. The Emperor ought to be attributed to the Hebrew letter *tzaddi* and the 28th path, whilst The Star should belong to the letter *Heh* and the 15th path. The reasons for this are not at all obvious to the uninitiated, but have been accepted as valid by most later commentators.

The most interesting aspect of all this lies in the fact that the centuries-old Tarot cards, which were probably devised as part of some heretical Gnostic system of belief back in the 12th or 13th centuries, have now come full circle and have been adopted by present day occultists practising methods of attainment which are in the main direct descendants of classical Gnosticism and neo-Platonism.[20]

6

THE ESOTERIC TAROT:
THE MINOR ARCANA

As DESCRIBED IN the previous chapter, A. E. Waite published a Tarot pack in 1910 which was based largely on the teachings of the Order of the Golden Dawn. In addition to the twenty-two major trumps, the Order had attributed the minor cards of the Tarot to the Qabalists' Tree of Life.

The minor cards of Waite's pack depicted certain aspects of these teachings and, furthermore, he used the Golden Dawn titles of the cards when deciding on their individual meanings in divination.

Most subsequent commentators have drawn on the same sources when explaining Tarot divination, so although the cards are known to have been used for this purpose as early as 1550,[1] the attributions assigned to each card today can largely be traced back to a system that was devised towards the close of the 19th century.

This present work includes a section on divination by Tarot cards, so it may be helpful to give a brief summary of how the Golden Dawn titles were arrived at.

First, the fifty-six cards were divided into two groups: the sixteen court cards and the forty numbered or "small" cards. Let us begin by examining the court cards.

THE COURT CARDS

These were attributed by the Golden Dawn to the four letters of the Divine name יהוה (Yod-Heh-Vau-Heh). In the process the sixteen cards underwent a considerable transformation from their traditional forms. They were now said to represent the various stages in the manifestation of force in the universe.

The first letter, Yod, symbolised primary energy, so to it were assigned the four cards which depicted "moving" figures, the Knights.

The second letter, Heh, showed the emergence of this energy into form, and was represented in the court cards by the four "maternal" figures, the Queens.

The third letter, Vau, showed the stabilisation of the process of formation, and was represented by the four "stable" cards, the enthroned Kings.

The fourth letter, Heh (final), revealed the completion of the movement of energy into form, and was symbolised by the four "children" of the Tarot, the Knaves or Pages.

As the Kings now came lower in the scheme than the Knights and Queens they were retitled "Princes", and in the pack created by the Golden Dawn for the use of its own members they were shown riding in chariots.

As a further innovation, so that the masculine/feminine polarity of the sequence might be clarified, the knaves were made into female figures and called "Princesses".

It might be argued that Qabalistically the alteration of the sequence King, Queen, Knight, Knave, into Knight, Queen, Prince, Princess makes sense, but it marks a drastic movement away from the traditional Tarot designs.

There is no historical evidence to support the claim that such changes serve to reconstruct the original Tarot pack which had already become corrupt before it was publicly known. Although there can be no intrinsic harm in experimenting with the cards by referring them to other systems of thought, such experiments cannot be justified on historical grounds.

Such claims apart, the Golden Dawn syncretic system makes a fascinating study. The titles of the sixteen court cards according to this system are given below because they throw light on the divinatory meanings of the cards, and because in many cases they are very evocative:

The suit of Batons
Knight: Lord of Flame and Lightning, King of the Spirits of Fire
Queen: Queen of the Thrones of Flames
King: Prince of the Chariot of Fire
Knave: Princess of the Shining Flame, Rose of the Palace of Fire

The suit of Cups
Knight: Lord of the Waves and the Waters, King of the Hosts of the Sea
Queen: Queen of the Thrones of the Waters
King: Prince of the Chariot of the Waters
Knave: Princess of the Waters and the Lotus

The suit of Swords
Knight: Lord of the Wind and the Breezes, King of the Spirits of the Air
Queen: Queen of the Thrones of the Air
King: Prince of the Chariot of the Wind
Knave: Princess of the Rushing Winds, Lotus of the Palace of Air

The suit of Coins
Knight: Lord of the Wide and Fertile Land, King of the Spirits of the Earth
Queen: Queen of the Thrones of Earth
King: Prince of the Chariot of Earth
Knave: Princess of the Echoing Hills, Rose of the Palace of Earth

THE SMALL CARDS

The forty numbered cards are divided equally between the four suits, so that each suit contains ten cards numbered from ace to ten. They were attributed by the Golden Dawn to the ten Sephiroth of the Tree of Life.

For example, the ace of each suit was linked with Sephirah 1, *Kether*; the deuce of each suit with Sephirah 2, *Chokmah*; the three of each suit with Sephirah 3, *Binah*, and so on down to the ten, linked with Sephirah 10, *Malkuth*.

As in the case of the court cards, the small cards were also attributed to the letters of the Divine Name, but this time according to suit: Batons with the letter Yod, the flaming torch of primal energy; Cups with the first letter Heh, the reception of energy in the vessel of form; Swords with the letter Vau, the establishment of form; Coins with the second letter Heh, the full material expression of that form.

A title suggesting the symbolic meaning of each card was

arrived at by correlating its position on the Tree of Life with the significance of its suit in terms of the Divine Name.

The way in which this was done is not at all obvious to anyone lacking a fairly close familiarity with the Qabalah, but the forty titles are given below because they form the basis of the divinatory meanings of the cards which appear in the next chapter.

They are also useful as keywords which can help in the process of memorising the full meanings.

The four aces, being assigned to the highest sphere on the Tree, were attributed to the four elements: Fire (Batons), Water (Cups), Air (Swords), and Earth (Coins). These elements symbolise, in traditional alchemical and hermetic lore, the first stage in the evolution of Prime Matter, the material from which the universe was originally created. The aces are therefore designated the "Roots of the Powers of the Elements".

The suit of Batons
1 Fire
2 Dominion
3 Established Strength
4 Perfected Work
5 Strife
6 Victory
7 Valour
8 Swiftness
9 Great Strength
10 Oppression

The suit of Cups
1 Water
2 Love
3 Abundance
4 Blended Pleasure
5 Loss in Pleasure
6 Pleasure
7 Illusionary Success
8 Abandoned Success
9 Material Happiness
10 Perpetual Success

The suit of Swords
1 Air
2 Peace Restored
3 Sorrow
4 Rest from Strife
5 Defeat
6 Earned Success
7 Unstable Effort
8 Shortened Force
9 Despair and Cruelty
10 Ruin

The suit of Coins
1 Earth
2 Harmonious Change
3 Material Works
4 Earthly Power
5 Material Trouble
6 Material Success
7 Success Unfulfilled
8 Prudence
9 Material Gain
10 Wealth

7

DIVINATORY MEANINGS OF THE MINOR ARCANA

IN THIS CHAPTER you will find the meanings, upright and reversed, of each of the fifty-six cards of the Tarot minor arcana. These meanings have been arrived at according to the system devised by the Order of the Golden Dawn.

This system, although of relatively recent origin, seems both balanced and comprehensive in its scope, and, it is claimed, has proved itself to be detailed and accurate in its results.

Whether or not one accepts the validity of the Golden Dawn scheme, or the possibility of accurate divination of any kind, the interpretations allocated to the various cards form a fascinating study in themselves. The meanings of the cards either individually or in combination can be made to cover practically any set of circumstances.

First we will deal with the meanings of the sixteen court cards. These are said to represent not situations or events, but people. When one of these cards appears it indicates someone of importance whose influence will have a bearing on future actions.

Each card reveals its positive, helpful aspect when it appears upright, and its negative, dangerous side when it appears reversed. It can therefore indicate possible assistance, protection or sympathy from someone, or else warn of treachery, misunderstanding or rejection.

The description of each card gives details of its traditional symbolism, as shown, for example, in the 19th century cards reproduced opposite page 220.

KING OF BATONS

Traditional appearance:

He is traditionally depicted as a clean-shaven man with long hair falling down to his shoulders. He wears a broad-brimmed hat resembling the figure-of-eight shaped hat worn by the Magician and Fortitude in old packs. The hat is surmounted by a golden crown, and he carries a long staff of office in his right hand. He is generally shown wearing armour, and is seated on a wooden throne.

Divinatory meanings:

Upright: A man who is noble and courageous, and who exhibits qualities of great strength and fortitude. He is virile and passionate, and has a loyal and generous nature. He is a lover of traditional ways and family life. He tends to act swiftly when provoked, yet on occasion may find it hard to be decisive because his essentially just outlook enables him to see every side of a problem. He often acts as a mediator, and is splendid at giving moral support.

Reversed: He is autocratic, ascetic, lacking in feeling for others, deeply prejudiced, ruthless in attaining his own ends, virtuous according to his own code, ethical in a narrow, intolerant fashion.

QUEEN OF BATONS

Traditional appearance:

A mature woman supporting a large green or yellow club against her right shoulder. She wears a crown and a flowing cloak and her long hair falls down her back and over her arms. Sometimes she is depicted wearing a topless gown which exposes her breasts. She is seated, but the details of her throne or chair are hidden behind her.

Divinatory meanings:

Upright: She is fertile both physically and mentally. She is by nature kind and sympathetic, friendly, generous and loving. She is a lover of the countryside and the works of nature, and is devoted to her home. She has a sound grasp of practical affairs, and is capable of independent thought and authoritative action. She is protective towards those within her circle. Her charm and social ease ensure her popularity.

Reversed: She is overbearing, matriarchal, unable to allow her loved ones independence of thought or action. She is vain and self-righteous, tending to take offence over imagined wrongs, and striking out at those who mean her no harm. She has a sharp tongue and a cruel wit.

KNIGHT OF BATONS

Traditional appearance:

A happily smiling young man rides a white horse, holding a roughly-hewn club upright at arms length as if about to present it to someone. He wears the familiar large floppy-brimmed hat and an armoured breast-plate. He does not display any weapons.

Divinatory meanings:

Upright: He is alert, active, swift-moving, unreasoning but highly intuitive. His movements are unpredictable and startling, but are generally seen to be wise in retrospect. He has an engaging temperament.

Reversed: He symbolises the wilful destruction of order, love of dispute and conflict for its own sake, premeditated arguments and deliberate sowing of the seeds of discontent.

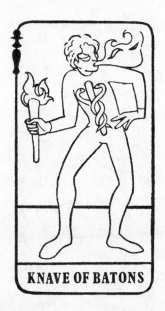

KNAVE OF BATONS

Traditional appearance:

A youth standing out of doors, supporting a massive upright club with both hands. He is shown in profile and wears a short tunic with a knee-length cloak over it. On his head is a floppy cap which sometimes has a tassel on the end, resembling that worn with Greek national costume.

Divinatory meanings:

Upright: He is ambitious and resourceful, enthusiastic and adaptable. He is a messenger who brings good tidings, stimulating news, witty gossip. He is by nature faithful and trustworthy, vigorous in the service of those in authority over him.

Reversed: He brings misleading information and slanderous gossip, and propagates scandal. He is unable to keep a secret, and will readily betray his trust. He is superficial whilst believing himself to be profound.

KING OF CUPS

Traditional appearance:

He is dressed in elegant robes and has a neatly trimmed beard. On his head is a broad-brimmed hat surmounted by an elaborate crown. He holds a large cup in his right hand, whilst his left arm rests casually on the side of his throne. He looks relaxed and confident.

Divinatory meanings:

Upright: He is skilled in the ways of the world. He is a born manipulator, gifted at conducting negotiations and arriving at a position of power and authority by means of the agility of his mind rather than the strength of his body. He is a man of ideas, a patron of the arts and sciences, an expert in law, and a leader in business. He seeks power and the fulfilment of his own high ambitions, and is adept at diverting the tides of fortune into channels that suit his own ends. He instinctively works in secret, behind the scenes, and avoids taking others into his confidence whenever possible. His motives remain hidden, and he is often distrusted or feared by those around him. He commands respect, but not love.

Reversed: He is treacherous, dishonest, caring only for himself, seeking always for the solution that is expedient. The only responsibility he feels is towards himself, and he has no moral sense. He involves those associated with him in evil, vice and scandal.

QUEEN OF CUPS

Traditional appearance:

She is dressed in a long flowing gown and sits on a throne which is sometimes canopied. In her right hand she holds a large cup which she supports on her knee. The cup is fitted with a lid. Her left hand grasps what might be a long-bladed knife or possibly a spatula. She has long hair and large, expressive eyes. In some packs she wears a close-fitting cap beneath her crown.

Divinatory meanings:

Upright: She is highly imaginative and artistically gifted, affectionate and romantic in outlook, and she creates an other-worldly atmosphere around herself. She is highly intuitive and her instincts can be trusted. She has an ethereal beauty which does not depend on external aids. She is easily influenced by events and the people she comes into contact with, and can become all things to all men. She evokes a happiness that is not dependent on earthly success.

Reversed: A dreamer who cannot be trusted. Her word is meaningless, as she changes her opinions and loyalties as the mood takes her. She is naturally perverse and can lead others to destruction in pursuit of some idle fantasy.

KNIGHT OF CUPS

Traditional appearance:

His long hair falls around his shoulders and he is bare-headed. He is dressed in a simple tunic and short cloak and rides a high-stepping brown horse. He holds a cup stretched out before him as if offering it to someone ahead. Sometimes he is shown with a chaplet of leaves around his brow.

Divinatory meanings:

Upright: He is enthusiastic, amiable, open to new ideas. He is a bringer of ideas, offers and opportunities. He is artistic and refined, but easily bored and in need of constant stimulation. He has high principles, but is easily led.

Reversed: False promises behind a fair countenance, duplicity and fraud. He shows an inability to discern where truth ends and falsehood begins.

KNAVE OF CUPS

Traditional appearance:

He walks slowly along a path, staring solemnly at the cup which he supports in the palm of his right hand. The top of the cup is generally covered by a fold of his cloak so that its contents are hidden. He wears a short tunic and is bare-headed, and sometimes carries a round cap in his left hand. In other versions a chaplet of small flowers encircles his head.

Divinatory meanings:

Upright: He is a poetic youth much given to quiet reflection and meditative study. He has a fund of useful knowledge and gives his advice freely when asked. He is painstaking and gifted with great foresight.

Reversed: He has much surface knowledge, but is essentially a jack-of-all-trades. He is selfish, seeking to keep what he knows to himself, and given to much quiet scheming. He has an appreciation of beauty but not enough application to become an artist.

KING OF SWORDS

Traditional appearance:

He is dressed in armour and grasps an upright sword in his hand. His left hand rests on the sheath that hangs at his side. Crescent moons adorn his shoulders and he is sitting on a simple plinth. On his head is a wide-brimmed hat surmounted by a crown.

Divinatory meanings:

Upright: He is mentally alert, inventive, of an original turn of mind, and is essentially rational in outlook. He is an advocate of law and order and an upholder of authority. He seeks executive office in order to see his ideas put into practice. Because of his versatility he often fails through lack of steady purpose; having formulated one plan he then proceeds to the next one with undue haste. He is an advocate of modernity at the expense of tradition.

Reversed: He is calculating, impersonal, deliberately cruel, even sadistic. He is capable of the utmost evil in pursuit of his intellectual goals. He may produce chaos in the name of order.

QUEEN OF SWORDS

Traditional appearance:

Like the king, she bears an upright sword in her right hand, but is not shown wearing armour. She wears simple, spartan clothes and is seated on an undecorated throne. She looks stern, and her left hand is often shown raised in warning. Her crown is light and unpretentious in appearance.

Divinatory meanings:

Upright: She is highly intelligent, has a complex personality, and is concerned with attention to detail and accuracy in all things. She is alert to the attitudes and opinions of those around her, and skilled at balancing opposing factions whilst she furthers her own schemes. She is self-reliant, swift-acting, versatile and inventive.

Reversed: She is devious, underhand, an expert in the use of the half-truth or quiet slander. Her subtlety and keenness of intellect make her a dangerous enemy.

KNIGHT OF SWORDS

Traditional appearance:

He is dressed in full armour and gallops forward on a spirited horse. He wears a plumed helmet and is often bearded. He brandishes a drawn sword in his left hand and gazes sternly ahead. His horse is richly caparisoned.

Divinatory meanings:

Upright: He is courageous, strong, highly skilled and at his best in a difficult situation. He indicates the approach of battles that must be fought and enemies who must be defeated by strength of arms. He is the archetypal warrior.

Reversed: He is headstrong, careless, heedless of warnings, impatient with details. He is fierce in action but has little staying power. He tends to start things which he cannot finish.

KNAVE OF SWORDS

Traditional appearance:

He is dressed in a full-sleeved tunic and flowing cloak. On his head is a wide-brimmed hat. He carries an upraised sword in one hand and rests the other on its scabbard. His general appearance is one of elegance and social ease.

Divinatory meanings:

Upright: He is vigilant and keen-sighted, and makes a good personal emissary. He is diplomatic and skilled in debate, and is able to discern the true nature of any affair, no matter how involved. He is an expert negotiator on behalf of his superiors.

Reversed: He is devious and given to prying into the affairs of others without good reason. He can be vindictive if crossed, and seeks out hidden weaknesses in his enemies whilst professing admiration and friendship for them.

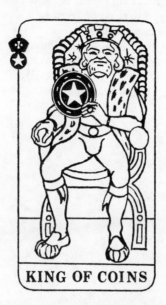

KING OF COINS

THE COURT CARDS: COINS

Traditional appearance:

He is seated on a low chair in the open air. He is bearded and dressed in heavy robes, with the familiar broad-brimmed hat on his head surmounted by a crown. Sometimes the crown appears simply as a design incorporated in his hat, at others it seems to be situated not on his head but balanced on the brim of his hat, at the back. He sits with one leg crossed casually over the other, and balances a large coin on his knee.

Divinatory meanings:

Upright: He is of a practical, down-to-earth nature; cautious, methodical, skilled in practical techniques and traditional crafts. He is loyal, trustworthy and patient. He has an inborn wisdom that enables him to achieve material success and even amass great wealth, despite his lack of imagination or intellectual deviousness. He is somewhat inarticulate, but is capable of deep thought along lines that engage his interest. He is slow to give affection, but devoted to those he loves; he is slow to anger, but implacable towards those he hates.

Reversed: He is dull, materialistic, impervious to beauty or refinement. He is unable to adapt to change, and remains committed to outmoded ways of acting and thinking long after they are generally dead. He is weak, servile, insular, easily bought.

QUEEN OF COINS

Traditional appearance:

She is dressed in gown and cloak, and is seated on a low-backed throne. She holds a large coin high in the air with her right hand, whilst her left arm cradles a sceptre. Her head is generally shown in profile and her crown is sometimes attached to the back of her headdress rather than resting squarely on top.

Divinatory meanings:

Upright: She is sensible, down-to-earth, wise and compassionate. She is a lover of comfort, splendour, ostentation, the grand occasion and the grand manner. She is lavish in her affection and her gifts, magnanimous and forgiving. She has a responsible attitude to her wealth, and uses it to support and advance those in her domain. She is not unduly intelligent or intuitive, but has a highly developed sense of feeling. She appreciates the good things of life.

Reversed: She is grasping, miserly, or else a spendthrift. She pours her wealth into new forms of display, extravagant luxury, overwhelming opulence. She is narrow in her outlook and suspicious of what she does not understand. She uses her power to surround herself with sycophants and shut out criticism or reproach. Her life is circumscribed by her material possessions and she is unable to rise above them.

KNIGHT OF COINS

Traditional appearance:

He rides slowly forward on a strong horse. He is dressed in the conventional broad-sleeved tunic and wears a close-fitting cap on his head. He displays a large coin in one hand and carries either a club or sceptre in the other.

Divinatory meanings:

Upright: He is the defender of what is generally thought right and true. He follows a high code of honour based on conventional standards. He is the upholder of tradition and age-old values. Patient in opposition, he relies for inspiration on established authority rather than his own judgement. He is a lover of practical virtues rather than abstract principles.

Reversed: He is the champion of an outmoded system against the forces of progress. He is complacent, smug, dull-witted and lacking in foresight.

157

KNAVE OF COINS

Traditional appearance:

He wears a tunic and broad-brimmed hat. He stands on open ground holding a large coin in his right hand, and rests his other hand on his hip. Sometimes a second coin is shown on the ground near his feet.

Divinatory meanings:

Upright: He is thrifty, conscientious, proud of the responsibility he carries. He is diligent in the performance of his duties and is essentially honourable. He has a sound business sense and makes a good administrator.

Reversed: He is idle, dull-witted, too meticulous, lacking in humour, full of a sense of his own importance. He enjoys wielding the degree of power that is his over those beneath him.

THE FORTY SMALL CARDS

On the following pages you will find the divinatory meanings of the remaining Tarot cards. These are arranged in suits: Batons first, then Cups, Swords, and finally Coins. The meanings of the cards will be seen to have been derived from their attribution to the Four Worlds of the Qabalists—the world of origination (Batons); the world of creation (Cups); the world of formation (Swords); and the world of sensation (Coins).

Accordingly, cards in the suit of Batons refer to matters of inspiration, ideas and intellect, and the exercise of will.

Cards in the suit of Cups refer to creation, love, feeling and all emotional matters.

Cards in the suit of Swords refer to movement, conflict, progress and the establishment of order.

Cards in the suit of Coins refer to material comfort, wealth, commerce and business, stability and security.

The cards therefore divide human existence into four main areas of endeavour, each of which is allotted ten cards that have one set of meanings when upright and another set when reversed.

In addition to its individual significance, each card can be interpreted further when combined with the cards flanking it in a spread, and when viewed as part of a group. This will be explained further in chapter 8, which is devoted to practical instruction in Tarot divination.

The illustrations depart from traditional Tarot design (see the plate opposite page 31) and instead depict images appropriate to the divinatory and esoteric meanings of each card.

ACE OF BATONS

Ace of Batons

Divinatory meanings:

Upright: Creativity, fertility, originality, conception, virility; the masculine, positive power of origination. The primal energy and vigour of the Element of Fire. The faculty of intuition. The natural fertility of nature. Indicates the beginning of something new, the launching of fresh enterprises, the foundation of future success and abundance. Also artistic inspiration, inventiveness, innovation.

Reversed: Impotence, barrenness, sterility; also pride, greed, avariciousness, over-confidence that ends in destruction.

TWO OF BATONS

Divinatory meanings:

Upright: Strength of will bringing ideas to pass. Firm rulership resulting in peace and justice. Riches and authority attained by just means. The responsible wielding of executive powers. Courage and initiative resulting from high motives. Earned success. Wisdom attained through experience.

Reversed: Ambition which will brook no obstacle, the will to power. Wealth attained by improper means. Pride without humility. Great success which ends in feelings of futility and emptiness. The achieving of a goal which turns out to be worthless. Loss of faith in oneself and one's motives.

THREE OF BATONS

Divinatory meanings:

Upright: The successful launching of a great venture. Original ideas finding expression. Inspiration which is being rewarded. Strength arising from enterprise and effort supported by powerful convictions. This is the card of the artist and the inventor who turns a dream into reality.

Reversed: Failure of nerve, inability to express ideas in tangible terms, pursuit of that which can never be. Indicates a lack of communication between the imagination and the physical world. Frustration with reality resulting in a retreat into fantasy. Grandiose schemes which can come to nothing. Failure to support ideas with practical means of expression.

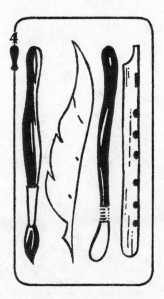

FOUR OF BATONS

Divinatory meanings:
Upright: Achievement in the realm of ideas. The card of the successful and renowned designer, innovator, or professional man. The establishment of beauty and elegance. Wit, mental alacrity, the most subtle arts of civilisation, refinement and culture.

Reversed: Decadence, extreme reliance on unnecessary etiquette and ceremonial. Lack of contact with the realities of life, leading to an existence bounded by artificial rules. Snobbishness and feelings of innate superiority based solely on tradition. Creative inspiration becoming hidebound and conventional.

FIVE OF BATONS

Divinatory meanings:

Upright: Opposition which requires mental agility to be defeated. Conflicts which cannot be avoided, tests that must be passed for further success to be attained or present achievement continued. Upheavals which call forth all resources of ingenuity and leave nothing secure. Indicates that the prize will have to be fought for relentlessly if it is to be gained.

Reversed: Avoidable litigation, fraud, defeat through trickery.

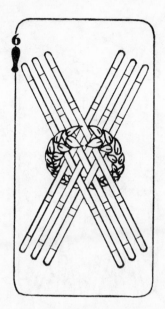

SIX OF BATONS

Divinatory meanings:

Upright: Victory, triumph, the arrival of great news. The complete fulfilment of major hopes and wishes. Success earned by hard work and originality, satisfaction in what has been achieved. The skilful overcoming of all opposition through the use of diplomacy instead of force.

Reversed: News delayed, fears about the outcome of any matter, apprehension regarding the hidden activities of enemies.

SEVEN OF BATONS

Divinatory meanings:

Upright: Indicates a time of great possibility which requires the exercise of courage and determination if it is to be realised. Points to powerful competition, but victory through sustained effort. Triumph over the vicissitudes of fate through personal valour. Opposition, obstacles, adversities, but the promise that success is within reach.

Reversed: Indecisiveness, timidity in the face of a challenge which leads to defeat. Hesitation will result in the loss of an opportunity. Exposure resulting in embarrassment, the calling of a bluff.

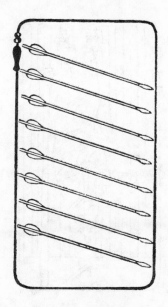

EIGHT OF BATONS

Divinatory meanings:

Upright: Hopeful change, movement, activity. The ending of delays and the speeding-up of all matters. Suggests a suitable time for taking the initiative, acting with courage and self-confidence, and grasping opportunities as they occur. A favourable omen for news and communications of all kinds, the promotion of understanding and co-operation. Important journeys are shown—particularly travel overseas or to a new country. This is not a card that indicates success in itself, but it suggests conditions which can lead to success.

Reversed: Brilliance, eloquence, or driving energy which are all dissipated and exhausted too quickly to have effect. Impetuous action by one who rushes ahead without first examining the terrain, and is therefore misapplied and wasted.

NINE OF BATONS

Divinatory meanings:

Upright: Great strength and stability which cannot be overthrown. Courage in defence and victory in attack. Assurance that opposition will be defeated. Reveals that one is in a safe and secure position which is unassailable.

Reversed: Obstinacy, inability to compromise, avoidable delays, suspicion, lack of adaptability.

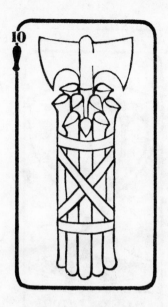

TEN OF BATONS

Divinatory meanings:

Upright: The triumph of force. Great good fortune which has become the means of oppression. Obstinacy and fixed ideas which serve to repress society into a static mould. Power which has no end beyond the expression of itself. The burden imposed by a surfeit of success.

Reserved: Deceit, guile, lies, all designed to disrupt the ordered affairs of others.

ACE OF CUPS

ACE OF CUPS

Divinatory meanings:

Upright: The feminine, passive power of gestation. The primal quiescence of the Element of Water. Nourishment, protection, the processes of creation, faithfulness, the faculty of feeling. Great fruitfulness is indicated, also fertility and the workings of love in the world. Can predict marriage, future motherhood, joy and plenty.

Reversed: Barrenness, the failure of love, stagnation, despair, loss of faith.

TWO OF CUPS

Divinatory meanings:

Upright: Love, emotional affinity, understanding, sympathy, joyous harmony, the reconciliation of opposites in mutual trust and fealty. Friendship, co-operation, the signing of a treaty, the end of a feud or rivalry, the resolving of arguments in happy agreement.

Reversed: Dissent, separation, divorce, deceit or unfaithfulness in a personal relationship. The throwing away of a valuable gift, the betrayal of trust. Also jealousy, vindictiveness, irresponsible revealing of the affairs of another.

THREE OF CUPS

Divinatory meanings:

Upright: Great happiness resulting from a marriage or a birth. The coming to fruition of something which was conceived in love. The card of maternity, abundant fertility, comfort, solicitation, trust, harmony, felicity and the healing of ills.

Reversed: Unbridled passion, sex without love, self-indulgence, sensuality, famine, illness, the selfish exploitation of the affections of others.

FOUR OF CUPS

Divinatory meanings:

Upright: Emotional happiness and fulfilment which has reached its peak and can proceed no further. The establishment of a family. The passive enjoyment of that which has already been attained. But the card also indicates a new dissatisfaction which the things of this world cannot assuage. Fulfilment having been attained, what can follow? Love is perhaps turning into familiarity.

Reversed: Satiety, excesses of all kinds. Fatigue or ill-health resulting from over-indulgence.

FIVE OF CUPS

Divinatory meanings:

Upright: The cup of happiness is overturned, harmony is replaced by worry and a sense of loss. Melancholy and disappointment are indicated here, yet though something is taken, alternatives remain to be explored. Indicates a need for a reassessment of one's life, followed by a major re-structuring. If this can be done, then all is not lost.

Reversed: Ill-luck which leaves one feeling bereft and impotent. Worries and anxieties which arrive unexpectedly.

SIX OF CUPS

Divinatory meanings:

Upright: Happiness built on past efforts. Harmony, well-being, pleasant memories and the realisation of a dream. Things of the past bringing pleasure in the present. The card also indicates new elements entering one's life which are linked in some strange **way** with the past, but which cause a renewal of activity in the present. The past, working through the present, will create the future.

Reversed: Nostalgia, and constant hankering after that which **is** gone and can never return. Failure through an inability to adapt to changing conditions.

SEVEN OF CUPS

Divinatory meanings:

   Upright: A card of choice. The enquirer is faced with several alternatives, one of which is of exceptional promise. But great perception is needed for this to be seen. The suggestion here is to examine one's aims and goals carefully if a major error of judgement is to be avoided. The Seven of Cups also sometimes indicates mystical experience of an inspiring kind.

   Reversed: Self-delusion, fantasy, reliance on false hopes. Opportunity lost through inaction. Deception in matters of love.

EIGHT OF CUPS

Divinatory meanings:

Upright: Changes in the sphere of the affections. The severing of links with the past which have outlived their relevance. A turning away from established relationships and objects of affection in order to progress to something new and deeper. Can indicate disillusion with the present which inaugurates the growth of greater contentment in the future. A change of viewpoint or perspective.

Reversed: Rejection of established love in favour of the pursuit of some impossible ideal. Restlessness and dissatisfaction which leads to the abandonment of that which has been well-founded.

NINE OF CUPS

Divinatory meanings:

   Upright: Emotional stability, contentment, a benign outlook, kindliness, liberality, generosity of spirit, feelings of well-being. Inner security which radiates a general aura of goodwill. An affectionate nature. Circumstances which foster these qualities.

   Reversed: Complacency, self-satisfaction, vanity, conceit, sentimentality, an overlooking of the faults in others which can lead to abuse of hospitality.

TEN OF CUPS

Divinatory meanings:

Upright: A peaceful and secure environment. The search for fulfilment is crowned with success. Perfect love and concord between people.

Reversed: Disruption of an ordered routine, anti-social actions, selfish exploitation of the goodwill of others. Manipulation of society for personal ends.

ACE OF SWORDS

Divinatory meanings:

Upright: Victory, success, triumph, the operation of irresistible force. The symbol of Divine justice and authority, the forging of strength in adversity. The faculty of thought. This card indicates that all enterprises will succeed, despite apparently overwhelming odds. The start of progress which cannot be halted or diverted. Necessary change; a breaking down in order that something better might be built. Freedom resulting from the removal of restraints.

Reversed: Wanton destruction, negative force, uncontrolled violence, power misused. Restriction imposed by force or fear. Injustice, the usurping of Divine authority by human will.

TWO OF SWORDS

Divinatory meanings:

Upright: Equilibrium, the interplay of the opposing forces of the universe which results in life. Truth and beauty arising from strife and dissent. Truce, peace and justice through the perfect balance of opposing arms or elements. Friendship in adversity.

Reversed: Love of tension and discord for its own sake. The deliberate stirring up of trouble. Trickery, deceit, betrayal, selfishness, the abuse of confidence, lack of self-control.

THREE OF SWORDS

Divinatory meanings:

Upright: Necessary strife and conflict. Destruction of that which is obsolete in order to clear the ground for what will come after. Disruption, upheaval, separation and discord, but all with a positive end in view—the establishment of something better.

Reversed: War, discord, strife, conflict, quarrels, enmity. Great disorder, either physical or mental. The breaking of a truce.

FOUR OF SWORDS

Divinatory meanings:

Upright: Peace and order established in the midst of strife through strength and the exercise of arms. Law and firm administration in troubled times. Rest and the opportunity to recuperate from the ravages of battle. A welcome retreat from the stresses of life. Can indicate necessary hospitalisation.

Reversed: Cowardice, a reluctance to face opposition. Exile, banishment, enforced seclusion, imprisonment, failure of nerve, depression.

FIVE OF SWORDS

Divinatory meanings:

Upright: Defeat, loss, dishonour, which cannot be overcome. The card implies that this must be accepted before future success in other directions can be achieved. Indicates a need to curb futile belligerence, swallow pride and accept the inevitable.

Reversed: Disaster as a result of weakness or indecision, malice, spite, treachery. Beware of someone acting in this fashion in your affairs.

SIX OF SWORDS

Divinatory meanings:

Upright: The solving of immediate problems, a moving away from imminent danger. Does not suggest complete success which absolves the need for further struggle, but indicates that some major obstacle had been overcome and progress can be resumed. May indicate travel away from trouble to more harmonious circumstances and surroundings.

Reversed: Success which is hardly won before further obstacles become apparent. Indicates a need for continuing effort and fortitude. Warns that attempts to escape from difficulties without solving them will not be successful.

SEVEN OF SWORDS

Divinatory meanings:

Upright: This card advises prudence and foresight when facing powerful opposition. Although a direct confrontation would be disastrous, victory can yet be attained by seeking out the enemy's weak points and disarming him in advance. But courage and perseverance are required. Great danger is stressed but also the possibility of triumph through cunning.

Reversed: Surrender when victory is almost attained, failure of nerve or effort, reluctance to carry through a daring course of action when it is needed.

EIGHT OF SWORDS

Divinatory meanings:

Upright: Restriction, major difficulties, enforced isolation and adverse circumstances dictated by fate. These can, however, be gradually overcome by patient effort and attention to detail. This card appears on the surface to be very unfortunate in meaning, yet serves to indicate that a cycle of adversity is coming to an end, and that changes for the better are already operating in one's life. But this is not an automatic process; opportunities must be grasped.

Reversed: Despair, frustration, depression, hard work with little reward. Misapplication of effort.

NINE OF SWORDS

Divinatory meanings:

Upright: Deception, disappointment, failure, cruelty, unreasoning passions, violence, scandal; all of which can be combated by resignation, passive obedience, faith and calculated inaction. This is the card of the martyr; it brings strength and new life out of suffering.

Reversed: Malice, misery, slander, complete isolation from help and comfort.

TEN OF SWORDS

Divinatory meanings:

Upright: Desolation, disruption and ruin—generally referring to a group or community rather than an individual. But cause for hope is suggested here. This card represents the nadir—the lowest point in this cycle of fortune. From now on things can only get better. The worst has already been experienced.

Reversed: The false dawn. An apparent lightening of burdens or release from affliction; but this will prove to be illusory or of temporary significance. The suffering will continue.

ACE OF COINS

A<small>CE OF</small> C<small>OINS</small>

Divinatory meanings:

Upright: Security, firm foundations, wealth, possessions, appreciation of physical beauty, sensuousness. The faculty of sensation. Material comfort, appreciation of the good things of life, the approach to the Spirit through the things of earth. The stability and luxury of the Element of Earth. Stoicism, the ability to endure adversity with steadfastness.

Reversed: Greed, avarice, miserliness, dependence on physical pleasures for happiness, materialism, lack of faith in anything beyond this world, fear of death, the pursuit of power and influence as ends in themselves. Lack of imagination or inability to alter fixed patterns of thinking or behaviour.

TWO OF COINS

Divinatory meanings:
Upright: The cycles of change at work in the world, the natural
fluctuations of fortune which must be allowed for when planning
ahead. Indicates movement and changes that are imminent—
news, communications, journeys, all connected with business,
money, material preoccupations. Stimulating developments which
give birth to an atmosphere of light-heartedness, laughter, joy in
the pleasures of society. Skilful navigation of the waters of
existence, knowledgeable manipulation of the rules of life to attain
continuing success.

Reversed: Reckless elation, foolhardy discounting of warnings of
impending trouble. Loss of opportunities for future success
through concentration on the pleasures of the moment. Unstable

effort, inability to carry ideas or projects through to a successful conclusion. Inconsistency of action which negates possibilities of success. Can indicate drunkenness or over-indulgence in physical pleasures.

THREE OF COINS

Divinatory meanings:

Upright: Successful progress in commercial and business ventures. The building up of future prosperity through originality and consistent effort. This is the card of the businessman, the merchant, and the craftsman. Rewards given to skill exercised at the right time. Indicates the success of any project commenced at this time, also the praise and appreciation of those whose opinion matters. Help and co-operation in commercial enterprises is indicated, and the establishment of a dynasty on firm foundations.

Reversed: Effort which results in disappointment and failure. Just criticism from those one respects. Obstinacy in the face of a need to desist. Conceit or prejudice which makes one unable to benefit from the advice or experience of others.

FOUR OF COINS

Divinatory meanings:

Upright: Complete material stability. The establishment of a financial or commercial empire. Triumph and the assumption of authority in business. Power achieved through acquisition of goods and possessions. The card indicates that monetary problems will be overcome and obstacles to business success removed. It shows law and order achieved through commercial transactions and peaceful negotiations rather than the imposition of force.

Reversed: Covetousness, an inability to delegate authority, over-centralisation of power and resources, bureaucratic methods which destroy individual initiative. Opposition to change for fear of loss of what has been established.

FIVE OF COINS

Divinatory meanings:

Upright: Poverty, destitution, material worries, unemployment, loss of security. This card warns of severe material adversities ahead, but suggests that enforced restriction in one area of life may open up possibilities in others. Important bonds may be formed with those in similar circumstances, and avenues still remain to be explored. The message here is "do not despair".

Reversed: Adversity which could be escaped from were it not for obstinacy and lack of imagination. Indicates that determination to proceed along a current path can only bring ruin, never success.

SIX OF COINS

Divinatory meanings:

Upright: Balance and solvency in material affairs. Income equals expenditure and the wheels of commerce turn smoothly. This is the card of the philanthropist, who uses his wealth not to build himself up, but to help others rise in the world also. It indicates charity, sympathy, kindness of heart, and the gratitude of one who has been well-favoured by fortune. Gifts, awards, help from above, patronage.

Reversed: Prodigality, carelessness with money, loss through theft or deceit, wealth used for self-aggrandisement and the acquisition of personal possessions.

SEVEN OF COINS

Divinatory meanings:

Upright: Possible material success, but inertia must be combated if it is to be grasped. Indicates that efforts made in the past may be wasted through inaction in the present. A warning that loss and disappointment are imminent; swift action must be taken to retain the fruit of one's labours. But all is not yet lost—good fortune is still possible.

Reversed: Loss, abandonment, monetary worries that are self-induced, promising circumstances that end in failure.

EIGHT OF COINS

Divinatory meanings:

Upright: Advantageous change in material circumstances. The turning of skills to ends which are satisfying and profitable. Labour bringing its reward. Indicates a time when efforts should be extended to bring about lasting success in the future. An auspicious card for anyone with talent or energy.

Reversed: A concentration on immediate returns at the expense of long-term success. The misuse of skill, dishonesty in business affairs. Diversion of opportunities into improper ends.

NINE OF COINS

Divinatory meanings:

Upright: Material success, comfort, appreciation, popularity. Good sense and sound administrative ability which produces order out of chaos.

Reversed: Prosperity gained by devious means, success which rests on the misfortunes of others. A warning that present stability will not endure for long.

TEN OF COINS

Divinatory meanings:

Upright: Inheritance, family wealth, blood ties. Prosperity built up through successive generations. Material security founded on the labours of one ancestors. Can indicate good fortune regarding a will or dowry. The establishment of a family tradition.

Reversed: The restricting effects of long tradition. Problems regarding legitimacy and lines of succession. Burglary, or the breaking-up of an estate after a death.

8

HOW TO CONSULT THE TAROT

Is there anything in it?

TAROT CARDS ARE known to have been used for divination during most, if not all, of their history. A book was published in Venice in 1550 which described the use of cards in gaining the answers to various questions, and when the Gypsies adopted the Tarot pack—probably in the second half of the 15th century—they seem to have used it as a method of fortune-telling from the very start.

This aspect of their history is probably one of the main reasons why they have survived largely unchanged down to the present day. Certainly they would not be known at all outside the Romance countries if it were not for their fame as shrines of mysterious occult wisdom and the secrets of the future.

Whether the persistent belief in Tarot cards as a reliable oracle has any foundation in fact is a subject which is not open to rational argument. Present-day science does not recognise any physical laws which could account for a correlation between a sequence of cards shuffled at random, and the occurrence of events in the future.

But intelligent and responsible people have asserted that in their experience such a thing is possible. Jung, for example, researched several methods of divination, including astrology and the Chinese I Ching, and his findings led him to develop his "theory of synchronicity" which, stated briefly, claims that all events occurring in a certain moment of time exhibit the unique qualities of that moment of time.[1]

This means that the moment of a person's birth is meaningfully linked with all other natural phenomena occurring at that moment, including the positions of sun, moon and planets in the sky.

Therefore a horoscope—a map of the Heavens as viewed from a particular point on the surface of the earth—erected for the time and place of the birth, will give the trained astrologer insights into the character and destiny of that person.

In the same way, when the I Ching is consulted by manipulating yarrow stalks as a question is being asked, the parts of the text which are arrived at as a result will give a relevant answer to the question.

Jung's theory can be applied equally well to the Tarot cards. In Tarot divination the cards are first shuffled, then laid out in various spreads, and interpreted by the reader.

Whether one accepts or rejects the theory of synchronicity is purely a matter of personal inclination and experience, though it would perhaps be unwise to reject anything so potentially useful without first giving it a fair trial.

When Sir Isaac Newton was upbraided by the then Astronomer Royal for his professed belief in astrology, Newton's reply was: "I, Sir, have studied the subject—you have not." Bearing this in mind, here is a guide to consulting the Tarot cards.

How to begin

Old traditions tell us much about how Tarot cards should be handled. Such customs can of course be ignored, but to do so would not be in keeping with the spirit of the Tarot, which must be approached in a sympathetic manner if it is to function.

Never allow your Tarot cards to be handled casually by the curious. The only time other hands touch the cards should be when they are being shuffled just prior to a reading.

You yourself should handle the cards as frequently as possible, studying the designs and imprinting their significance on your memory. The more you are familiar with the cards, it is said, the better they will work for you. This is for two reasons:

First, Tarot divination can only work if you have built a bridge of intuition between your subconscious mind and the symbols of the cards—this takes time.

Second, the cards must become imbued with what one might call your personal vibrations. A kind of rapport must be created between you and your personal pack of Tarot cards. Any experienced reader will tell you that a new pack must be broken in by frequent handling before it will give reliable results.

Casual handling of the cards by hands other than your own will swiftly break down the link you have forged with them.

This question of protecting the cards from outside influences is a very important one, which is stressed in all traditional instructions regarding the use of the Tarot, and which is found in magical systems in all parts of the world. The setting apart of a ritual object is thought to keep its special powers and qualities intact.

Many Hindu yogis, for example, can only exhibit paranormal faculties when seated on a mat woven from certain grasses which are believed to insulate the body from the magnetic currents of the earth. There is no known scientific foundation for such a belief, so perhaps the "setting apart" is a necessary part of the training of consciousness to exercise its lesser-known abilities, and the effect is psychological. If you believe a thing is sacred then it becomes imbued with the power of the psyche and can act as a focal point for the display of psychic phenomena.

When your Tarot cards are not being used, you should wrap them in a square of silk, preferably purple or black in colour. The pack should be kept in its silk covering inside a wooden box fitted with a lid, which should then be stored in a place where other people are unlikely to handle it—if possible on the side of the room that faces east, the direction from which light and inspiration symbolically appear.

You also need a flat surface on which to lay the cards when reading them, sufficiently large to accommodate all the cards needed for the largest spread—about two feet square is the smallest practicable size.

Commencing a reading

To achieve a suitable atmosphere in the reading room it helps to commence by lighting some incense or a joss-stick. This can put you and the querent (the name given to the person for whom you are giving the reading) in a calm, receptive frame of mind.

Then open the box and take out the Tarot cards wrapped in their silk cover, and place them—still enclosed in the silk—at the centre of the table.

Ask the querent to sit at the table on the south side facing north. Seat yourself on the north side of the table facing south. This is because, in esoteric lore, the hidden currents of the earth are said to flow from north to south and back again, and therefore the seat of authority and power is in the north. (In ancient China magistrates always sat at the north end of an audience chamber, with litigants facing them from the south.)

If you are reading the cards alone, either for yourself or for someone who is absent, then sit facing the east.

You are now ready to start the reading. Take the cards from their wrapper of silk, which should be spread flat across the table. The square of silk should be sufficiently large to cover the area of a spread, so that as each card is dealt it can be placed on the silk and thus avoid contact with the table-top.

These rather elaborate preparations may appear to be a superstitious irrelevance, but they do serve to concentrate the mind on what is being done, and awaken whatever psychic faculties may be present.

There are a vast number of Tarot spreads. Here are three. The Nine Card Spread relates to the past, present and future; the Circular Spread forecasts the year ahead, and the Horseshoe Spread deals with a specific question.

In every case the reader shuffles the cards thoroughly, turning some of them from top to bottom at intervals to ensure that there will be a mixture of upright and reversed cards by the time the shuffling is completed.

The reader hands the shuffled pack to the querent requesting him or her as the case may be to shuffle them again in the same fashion, remembering to reverse some of the cards.

The reader then takes the pack from the querent and begins laying out whichever spread seems most appropriate to the querent's needs.

The Nine Card Spread

The cards having been shuffled by you and the querent as described above, take the pack from the querent, face downwards, and deal nine cards from the top, laying them on the table in the order and pattern shown in Diagram A, still *face downwards*.

Now turn card No. 1 face upwards. This card indicates the most salient feature of the querent's present circumstances. Interpret the card from this angle.

Next, turn card No. 2 face upwards. This card indicates the highest that the querent can attain at this time.

Turn card No. 3 face upwards. This indicates hidden or subconscious factors that are operating in the querent's affairs; the background to the present situation.

Turn card No. 4 face upwards. This card reveals past causes of the present situation.

Turn card No. 5 face upwards. This indicates the probable outcome if prevailing trends are carried through unchanged; not necessarily what *will* happen, but what is probable if no major influences are brought to bear on the course of events.

Cards Nos. 6 to 9 inclusive give a brief outline of the querent's probable progress in the near future. The indications here are of a

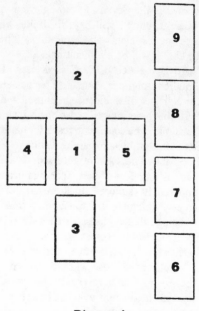

Diagram A

very general nature, and might extend over a period of weeks or months. They should be interpreted in sequence, card No. 6 showing events closest in time, and card No. 9 events furthest away.

This initial spread should be undertaken without any prior consultation between the reader and the querent. In this way the reader can gain a totally unbiased picture of the querent's present situation.

Here is a hypothetical reading using this spread which will give you an idea of how the cards are interpreted in practice, and how their meanings are linked together into a significant whole.

Assume that the first card you turned up was the Eight of Coins. This reveals that the querent is at a time when he can expect a change for the better to occur in his material affairs. The tides of fortune favour progress in his work or career, and he can expect opportunities to be offered to him. The general outlook is good.

The second card is the Seven of Cups. Several offers will be made to the querent, but he will have to decide which of these gives most scope for his talents and aspirations. The implication here is that the choice will be a difficult one.

The third card is the Ace of Wands reversed. Herein lies a warning. The querent might easily make a serious error of judgement, either through lack of confidence in himself and his abilities, or alternatively through an inflated sense of his own qualities and potential. He must have the courage to reach for his goal, yet at the same time be certain that his aims are realistic.

The fourth card is The Chariot reversed. It belongs to the major arcana, and is therefore of particular significance. It reveals either that the querent has suffered a major reversal of fortune in the past; just when everything seemed to be going smoothly, and his ambitions were being fulfilled, disaster struck. Or that the querent is one who has achieved his present success by exploiting others and furthering his own plans at their expense. Either of these interpretations would make sense when compared with the preceding card, the Ace of Wands reversed. The reader must decide, by his assessment of the querent who sits before him, and by the exercise of his intuition, which meaning is appropriate.

The fifth card is the Seven of Coins. The suggestion here is that the possible success shown in card one, the Eight of Coins, and card two, the Seven of Cups, may be missed through the querent failing to grasp what is offered him. Again, this may be through fear of failure, or due to pride and a false sense of his own importance. Success will not fall into his lap—he must reach out and take it.

The sixth card is the Three of Wands. A highly auspicious card which indicates the success of a major venture, the chance to use one's initiative and further an important plan. It shows the opportunity that the previous cards have pointed towards.

The seventh card is the Queen of Swords. The appearance of a King or Queen in a spread often indicates that the querent will be offered help or advice from someone answering that particular card's description. So, the querent in this instance (as the card is upright) will be offered sound advice or helped by a woman who has an incisive intellect and the ability to dive into the heart of a complex problem and come up with a quick and workable solution. The Queen of Swords also suggests, however, that she is not a lady who puts herself out for nothing, so she will expect something in return for her efforts.

The eighth card is the Eight of Batons. From this it seems that the pitfalls mentioned earlier will be avoided, as it promises the removal of obstacles, the furtherance of plans, and successful progress. Good news, and in particular travel, are also shown.

The ninth and final card is the Eight of Cups. Cards from the suit of Cups are generally said to refer to emotional matters, but often indicate changes in a person's attitudes to himself, to others, and to life in general. Here, the Eight of Cups shows that the querent will successfully overcome either the fear or the pride within himself which might be the cause of his downfall. As such it is an auspicious omen for the future.

At this stage in the reading, all nine cards of the spread lie face upwards before you. Summarise them briefly, and indicate once more the main points of their message to the querent.

In our hypothetical example of this Nine Card Spread the message is that the querent can expect opportunities to be offered him, but he is warned that he must either overcome his fears or swallow his pride (whichever you believe is appropriate) if he is not to make a serious blunder. He must forget the past and concentrate on the future. Good advice and help will be offered him by an intelligent woman, which he would be wise to take. If he does this, then all will be well.

The Circular Spread

The Circular Spread is one of the most reliable for giving a general forecast for the year ahead, beginning from the date of the readings.

When the cards have been shuffled by you and the querent and then returned to you, proceed as follows. Working from the top of the pack, lay out twelve cards *face upwards* in a circle, then lay

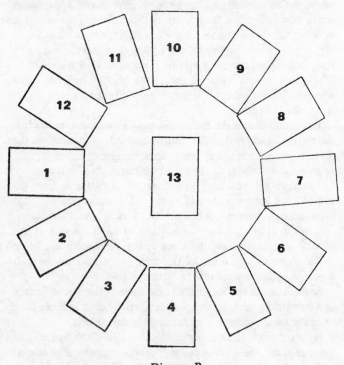

Diagram B

the thirteenth card face upwards in the middle of the circle as illustrated in Diagram B. This last card is most important as it gives the overall tone of the reading and the year ahead. Interpret it *first*.

Then interpret the twelve cards of the circle in sequence, moving in an anti-clockwise direction.

The example spread described below will help you to relate the cards to each other and to the querent's affairs. It will also help if you have a pack of Tarot cards to lay them out in this order and refer to them as you read this section. Out of the thirteen cards in this spread eleven are upright, with their tops towards the centre of the circle. The other two cards are reversed, with their bottoms towards the centre of the circle.

The card in the middle of the circle is No. 1, the Magician. His presence here indicates that this is a year in which the exercise of initiative and a willingness to take risks will result in success. This year will see the commencement of a new chapter in the querent's affairs.

The first card on the edge of the circle is the Ace of Batons. This refers to the months ahead and suggests that it is a good time for launching fresh enterprises which will bear sound fruit in the future.

The second card refers to conditions two months hence. Here is the Two of Cups, which shows that the querent will have to choose between attractive alternatives, and will need to be very discerning if he is to make the right decision.

The third card is The Hermit, a major arcana card that reveals an important stage in the querent's affairs three months ahead. It advises careful planning and profound thought before progress is attempted. Impatience at this point could be disastrous. Sound advice will be offered, either by another person, or by the promptings of the querent's own inner self.

The fourth card is the Six of Swords, which points to the successful resolution of current problems in the fourth month.

The fifth card is the King of Coins, which pictures a man who is practical, skilled in his work, and loyal to the querent. Someone of this nature will assume a position of importance in the querent's affairs in the fifth month.

The sixth card is the Nine of Batons, showing that the sixth month is an excellent time to act forcefully and so overcome major opposition. The querent may be hard pressed but his basic position will be secure and courage will bring victory.

The seventh card is the Three of Cups, reversed. Here is a serious warning that the querent will be in danger of losing what he has gained as a result of self-indulgence and a callous disregard for the rights of others.

The eighth card is the Four of Cups reversed, indicating fatigue or ill-health resulting from the excesses shown in the last card.

The ninth card is the Seven of Coins, pointing to loss of material possessions and security which have been built up over a long period of time, unless the querent pulls himself together. This card is a good omen in that it reveals that all is not yet lost, and a return to good fortune is still possible.

The tenth card is Fortitude, one of the Tarot major arcana. This is a card of decisive victory over undisciplined instincts and the control of irrational behaviour. It shows that the querent will successfully recover from the set-back described earlier.

The eleventh card is the Two of Cups, a symbol of the return of harmony and the resolving of tension and opposition.

The twelfth and final card is The Chariot, one of the major arcana, showing safe progress along one's destined path, the surmounting of all obstacles, and a personal triumph.

The Horseshoe Spread

When the answer to a specific question is desired, the Horseshoe Spread is simple yet comprehensive.

Having shuffled the cards, ask the querent to shuffle them, concentrating the while on his or her question.

Take the cards back from the querent, *face downwards*, and deal seven cards off the top of the pack, laying them on the table in the Horseshoe shape shown in Diagram C *face upwards*.

Read the cards in an anti-clockwise direction from left to right.

Card 1 refers to past influences.

Card 2 refers to the querent's present circumstances.

Card 3 refers to general future conditions.

Card 4 indicates the best policy for the querent to follow.

Card 5 reveals the attitudes of those around the querent.

Card 6 points to obstacles standing in the way of a solution to the querent's question.

Card 7 intimates the probable final outcome of the question.

Here is an example of an answer to a question provided by the Horseshoe spread. The question is asked by a woman who has been an innocent victim in a road crash, and is seeking compensation: "What will be the outcome of the legal case in which I am involved?"

Let us suppose that the cards fall as follows: The Tower, Ace of Cups, Nine of Cups, Seven of Batons, Three of Cups reversed, The Lovers, The Queen of Coins.

Here is a possible interpretation: The first card, The Tower, referring to the past, indicates that the querent has suffered a major set-back through no fault of her own.

The second card, the Ace of Cups suggests that the querent is now receiving the protection and support necessary for her recovery. As the question relates to a legal matter, this card could also be interpreted as meaning that the querent's affairs are being properly looked after by her legal advisers.

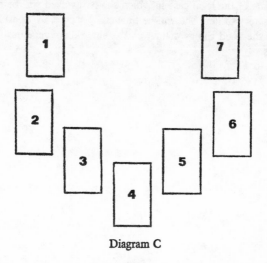

Diagram C

The third card, the Nine of Cups, forecasts that the querent's future is secure, that her peace of mind will be restored, emotional stability and happiness will be regained.

The fourth card, the Seven of Batons, advises her that courage and determination are still necessary to overcome opposition, but sustained effort will ensure victory.

The fifth card, the Three of Cups reversed shows that there are certain people around her who given the chance are likely to exploit her. She must take good care that this does not happen.

In the area representing the obstacles facing the querent stands the sixth card, The Lovers. This suggests that the querent will have a choice to make, and will be guided to the right decision by a flash of insight. It could mean that she will receive an offer from the opposing side to settle out of court, and she may accept this or press on to trial. Tracking back to the Seven of Wands, the guidance here suggests that if she is not altogether satisfied with the amount offered for an out of court settlement she should continue to fight. If on the other hand she is satisfied with the offer, she should accept it.

The seventh card, the Queen of Coins, gives the final answer to the querent and symbolises a happy solution to her question. The outcome of the legal case in which she is involved will be highly satisfactory to her. She will be financially secure, in a position to enjoy the good things of life, and to share them generously with others.

9

MEDITATION AND THE TAROT

IT IS BY no means unlikely that some of the heretical sects of Medieval Europe acquired knowledge of esoteric physical and mental disciplines from those Gnostic sources in the East which emerged from the same background as applied philosophies such as Tantric yoga.

The Tarot cards display a powerful array of psychic images, and it can be surmised that they were used not only as teaching aids but as focal points of consciousness during individual and group meditation.

The purpose of meditation is to concentrate attention on the level of symbolic consciousness which lies between the ego and the inner self. The powers of the unconscious cannot be contacted directly by the rational mind, but may be approached via the use of appropriate symbols.

Symbols can be thought of as psychic transmitters, which bring into focus the primordial images of the psyche and channel their power through into consciousness. They are the language by which the inner worlds make themselves known.

By a process of sustained concentration on the edges of the mind the appearance of such symbols can be both observed and studied. They are the seeds of new life which, if properly nurtured and cared for, can grow until they bear the fruits of fresh insights and enlarged awareness of the inner realities of the whole self.

They can act as stages on the way which leads to the hidden centre. But, untrained, they often emerge in an unformed and chaotic fashion—as in dreams—and to be of any value they must be recollected and disciplined into the context of some known symbolic system.

Jung found a solution to this problem by comparing the dreams and visions of his patients with the themes of mythology and alchemy. The meaningful parallels which he found as a result enabled him to place his subjects' experiences in an already known symbolic framework and thus discover their significance.

Meditation is a means of training the mind to use symbols as steps or gateways on a journey of exploration which leads from the egocentric field of the conscious mind through to the larger and richer domain of the higher self.[1]

This is the psychological significance of myths in which a hero descends into the underworld, defeats a monster, and claims the King's daughter for his bride; or in which he sacrifices himself, is killed, and is then reborn into a new and better life.[2]

The mythical quest is both difficult and dangerous, for death must precede rebirth—the ego must be transcended before the true self, the treasure hard to attain, can irradiate the personality.

One well-known example of a Western meditation-system is Ignatius Loyola's *Spiritual Exercises*.[3] Here, after a period of intense self-examination, the subject recreates in his imagination the experiences of Christ from the time of his passion through to his resurrection, projecting himself into the scenes described in the Stations of the Cross until he actively experiences the sufferings and triumph of his Lord.

This method of enhancing and revitalising consciousness through the skilled use of the creative imagination is analogous to the experiences undergone during initiation rituals of death and rebirth, the second half of the Jungian process of individuation, the operations of alchemy, and the images of the Tarot cycle.

The twenty-two cards of the Tarot major arcana have been used extensively by Western occultists during the past century as an important part of their Qabalistic 'Tree of Life' meditation system. As explained earlier (see Chapter 5) the cards are attributed to the twenty-two paths of the Tree and used as visualisation aids in 'rising on the planes'.

But they can be used effectively by themselves, without reference to any other system. Here are some indications of how this can be done.

The aim of Tarot meditation is to project oneself in the imagination into each card in turn, exploring its imagery, getting the 'feel' of its symbolism, uncovering its meaning in terms of one's own psychic structure.

We all differ in detail, both physically and psychologically, and so the message of each Tarot image will be personal to us, even though its broad significance is applicable to all.

For this reason, the study of another person's experiences and findings can only be of academic interest. What they have discovered is personal and significant to them; what you discover is personal and significant to you. The symbolism of the Tarot trumps is of sufficient richness and depth to enable everyone to unveil fresh insights and new possibilities as they journey along the way. They are a 'treasure-house of images' which can never be exhausted.

The cards should be worked on *in sequence*, starting with the unnumbered card The Fool and ending with card XXI The World. Each card leads on from the one preceding it, and prepares the way for the one which follows, so choosing cards at random can give misleading results.

A period of meditation can be for a short or long length of time, though for beginners short sessions of ten minutes or so are best until the mind gets used to its unusual activity.

Each session can be devoted to a single card, in which case it should be part of a programme of daily study extending over several weeks. Alternatively, it can take in the entire twenty-two card sequence, working through the cards one by one as the 'story' develops, reaches its climax, and is resolved.

It is not necessary to enter a trance-like state in which one becomes unaware of one's surroundings in order to meditate successfully. The aim should be to attain a degree of concentration in which surroundings do not distract from the inner vision being evoked.

Begin by sitting comfortably in a chair, breathe evenly and easily and relax. Gaze at the appropriate Tarot card which should be placed before you at a comfortable height and distance—propping the card upright on a table in front of you is probably the best way of achieving this.

After a few sessions you should be able to picture the card clearly in your mind's eye. At this point you should meditate with your eyes closed, which will heighten your concentration and also make the images live more vividly in your imagination.

The next step is to make the scene before you as real as possible. To do this, mentally clothe the figures and scenery in bright, living colours; endow them with weight and solidity so that you are no longer gazing at a flat, two-dimensional image, but looking through the border of the card as if through a window-frame or doorway on to a real scene beyond.

Now visualise yourself inside the scene. Step in your imagination over the threshold of the card as if through an open door, and stand with the characters in their own world.

When you have proceeded this far—and it will probably take several sessions of concentrated meditation before you can make a scene 'live' in this way—let your attention relax and see what happens. Perhaps nothing will occur the first few times you try this. But gradually you will find that new ideas regarding the significance of the images appear in your mind.

These may take the form of abstract thoughts which suggest fresh lines of enquiry. New symbols might be discovered in the scene which were not in the original Tarot design, or the characters might move and perform various actions or even speak, in which case you should listen and try to catch what is being said.

Visualise the characters as strongly as you can. See the breeze rustling their garments if they are out of doors, watch how they reveal their temperaments by the way they gesture and move. Smell the odours of grass or forest or barren desert; hear the sound of flowing water or moving feet.

After your period of meditation is over, note down or tape details of what you have experienced, even if nothing very important seemed to happen. Get into the habit of doing this every time you have completed your meditation, for it is through keeping a record that you can build up a picture of the motifs being presented to you. Symbols that rise from the depths of the unconscious through the portal of the Tarot images need to be interpreted. To do this it is necessary to study them over a period of time and see them in as wide a context as possible.

Striking visual images can be drawn, painted or modelled as an aid to memory and as a means of exploring them further. Verbal descriptions are often inadequate when describing powerful symbols.

It is important when you have finished your meditation that you "close down" properly. The powers which can be invoked during the visualisation process *must be dismissed thoroughly* before you return to everyday consciousness.

If you simply sit up and open your eyes, they may linger on and interfere with your normal concentration. To avoid this kind of psychic leakage, always end your meditation in the way you began it, but in reverse order.

Starting by retreating out of the visualised scene until you can see it framed before you in the outline of the card. Then halt the movement and reduce the bright colours and three-dimensional shapes until the scene becomes just a flat, lifeless drawing. When you are able to see just a printed design on a piece of card, you may open your eyes and consider the session at an end.

By building up a detailed account of your progress and discoveries over a period of weeks, months or even years you will gain a true and valuable insight into the inner significance of the mystical quest and its relevance to the realities of your personal psyche. Such a programme of meditation not only has a harmonising and therapeutic effect, but can lead in time to what some mystics have called the Knowledge and Companionship of the Holy Guardian Angel, which is the living presence of the inner self.

Below you will find detailed descriptions, including colours, of the twenty-two major trumps as depicted in the drawings which illustrate Chapter 4. These were prepared specially for this book as clear, usable interpretations of the Tarot images. By basing your meditations on the drawings and the descriptions of them given here you should be able to develop your powers of visualisation with minimum difficulty.

You will see that each card is assigned either one or two titles in addition to its main, traditional title. These subsidiary titles were originally devised by the Order of the Golden Dawn as part of its Tree of Life meditation system, but have proved to be so evocative that they have passed into the general body of esoteric tradition. You may find them of considerable help when analysing the deeper significance of the cards.

O. *The Fool*. The Spirit of Ether.

A fair-haired youth is seen wearing a richly decorated costume of green and gold. He skips happily along his way, his eyes fixed on a silver butterfly which flutters before his face. He seems unaware of the cliff-face looming beneath his feet, or of the dog savagely biting his left leg—perhaps in warning. Over his right shoulder he carries a satchel made of indigo leather, suspended from an ebony wand which he grasps in his left hand. From his right hand dangles a white rose, and more white roses are visible behind him, growing amongst the fresh springtime grass. The sun can be seen over his shoulder, shining in the pale blue morning sky.

I. *The Magician*. The Magus of Power.

A young man with an expression of calm self-assurance on his face stands before an open-air altar. His long dark hair flows flame-like around his head, and his scarlet cloak flares out from his body as if charged with power. His left hand holds aloft a flaming sceptre and his right hand points to the altar before him. On the altar lie a chalice, a wand, a sword and a disc or pantacle. Red roses and white lilies blossom at his feet. His inner garments are of a brilliant whiteness, contrasting with the scarlet of his cloak and girdle. Above his head is suspended a horizontal figure eight, the symbol of the eternal.

II. *The Papess*. The Priestess of the Silver Star.

A beautiful, ethereal woman is seen, dressed in flowing robes of silver and blue which appear to dissolve into water at her feet. She wears a tall, crowned headdress and a large book lies open on her lap. She is seated upon a throne backed by an aquamarine silk curtain, which stands between two pillars that have capitals carved to resemble lotus buds. The pillar on her right is white and the pillar on her left is black.

III. *The Empress*. Daughter of the Mighty Ones.

A dignified woman is seated out of doors amidst luxurious surroundings. She is wearing a rose-pink gown and a crown of myrtle encircles her golden hair. Twelve silver stars shine in a circle above her head. In her left hand she holds an ear of corn, and her right hand rests on a golden cornucopia from which pours a stream of many-coloured fruits. At her feet lies an emerald green shield, bearing the device of a cherry-red eagle. Behind her is a waterfall, and the warm summer sun floats in the blue sky above a verdant forest.

IV. *The Emperor.* Son of the Morning, Chief among the Mighty.

A powerfully-built man, bearded and dressed in rich robes of crimson and purple, sits out of doors on a golden throne which bears the device of a black eagle on a cerise ground. He wears steel armour beneath his robes, and on his head he bears a heavy iron crown. His left hand grasps a jade-green sceptre, whilst in his right hand he holds a golden orb surmounted by a Maltese Cross. Behind him can be seen a hot, mountainous, desert landscape.

V. *The Pope.* Magus of the Eternal Gods.

A dignified, patriarchal figure, robed in heavy gold and maroon vestments is seen enthroned in his audience room. On his head he wears a Papal crown of gold, decorated with three rows of red trefoils. His hands are encased in white gloves; the right hand raised in the sign of benediction and the left hand holding a triple-tiered crucifix. Before the Pope kneel two tonsured priests. The one on his left is robed in white, the one on his right in crimson. Behind him, merging into the gloom, can be seen two heavy stone pillars.

VI. *The Lovers.* Children of the Voice Divine, the Oracles of the Mighty Gods.

A group of three people, a man and two women, stand on a grassy bank. Above them the figure of Eros is seen appearing from a cloud, aiming his arrow at the young man who stands beneath him. The youth, dressed in garments of blue and silver, looks towards the mature, dark-haired woman on his right, but his body inclines towards the fair-haired maiden on his left. The older woman, dressed in robes of purple and gold, places her hand on the young man's shoulder. The young woman, in a gown of green and turquoise, waits demurely with downcast eyes.

VII. *The Chariot*. Child of the Power of the Waters, Lord of the Triumph of Light.

A proud young hero dressed in golden armour stands erect in his chariot, being drawn along by a strange two-headed beast. Silver crescents adorn his shoulders and a fleur-de-lys is engraved on his breastplate. On his head is a golden crown and he grasps a flaming scarlet sceptre in his right hand. The chariot has red wheels and a blue canopy embroidered with stars which is supported by four wooden pillars. The charioteer is surrounded by yellow light, as if he is emerging from the sun.

VIII. *Justice*. Daughter of the Lord of Truth, the Holder of the Balances.

An authoratitive woman is seen seated squarely on a throne. Her right hand holds aloft a large two-edged sword, and from her left hand hangs a pair of golden scales. She is dressed in a heavy robe of a cool green colour, beneath which can be seen a dark blue gown. A heavy crown sits on her head and her feet are shod in golden slippers. The back of her throne is composed of two wooden pillars, between which hangs a violet curtain.

IX. *The Hermit*. The Magus of the Voice of Light, the Prophet of the Gods.

An elderly, bearded man moves slowly along a poorly lit and stony path. He is dressed in brown garments resembling a monk's habit. The way before him is lit by the lantern which he carries

---

Six court cards from an early 19th-century pack produced by Teodoro Dotti, Milan. These cards are finely engraved and coloured, and follow the traditional designs quite closely, as shown in the postures of the figures and details of their dress. In the Queen of Coins (*Reg. di Danari*) for example, the Queen's crown is situated on the back of her head rather than being placed squarely on top—a convention which appears on the earliest surviving examples of Tarot cards. (British Museum: Willshire collection.)

RE DI COPPE

REG. DI COPPE

REG. DI DANARI

RE DI SPADE

CAVAL. DI BASTONI

FANTE DI BASTONI

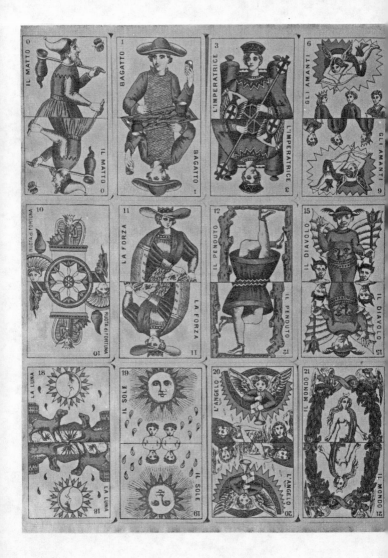

in his right hand, shielded by his sleeve from the force of the wind. His left hand grasps a heavy staff, around which is entwined a serpent. Although his cloak is hooded, the hood is thrown back and his head is bare.

X. *The Wheel of Fortune.* The Lord of the Forces of Life.

A multi-coloured wheel with eight spokes hangs from a twin-pillared frame of wood. On the grass that sprouts beneath the wheel squats a monkey, whilst above the wheel presides a fiery dragon bearing an upright sword. On the right of the wheel, ascending, hangs a blue, dog-like creature, whilst from the left of the wheel, descending, is suspended a strange creature of crimson hue. Behind the wheel can be seen a deep violet sky.

XI. *Fortitude.* Daughter of the Flaming Sword, Leader of the Lion.

A calm, confident young woman dressed in flowing robes of blue and amber gently but firmly grasps the jaws of a powerful red lion that crouches before her. On her head is a large and curiously-shaped black hat, whilst from her shoulders hang the folds of a voluminous dark red cloak. In the background can be seen a forest and mountains are visible in the distance.

XII. *The Hanged Man.* The Spirit of the Mighty Waters.

A young man hangs upside-down in the air, suspended by his

Twelve major trump cards from a modern Italian pack produced by the firm of Masenghini, Bergamo. These, like all present-day Italian cards, are double-headed and are primarily intended for playing card games. Although much of the original symbolism has been lost, interesting details can still be seen. The Fool (*Il Matto*) is shown carrying a butterfly net and is in pursuit of his prey. The Magician is called *Bagatto*, "The Cobbler", and an array of shoe-mender's tools can be seen on the bench before him. Fortitude (*La Forza*) wears the curious figure-of-eight shaped hat which occurs frequently in Tarot designs. The Devil (*Il Diavolo*) wears a horned helmet and has the head of a fierce beast drawn across the front of his tunic. The dancer in the middle of The World (*Il Mondo*) has a crescent moon poised on her head. (Author's collection.)

left ankle from a wooden gibbet. His facial expression is not one of suffering, however, but reveals calm detachment, and his head is surrounded by a halo of golden flame. His hands appear to be tied behind his back, and his right leg hangs loosely behind his left. His left ankle is bound not with a rope but with a supple branch of the gibbet cross-piece. He is dressed in a deep blue jacket secured by seven silver buttons, and red hose. The gibbet is bright green in colour, suggesting that it is made from living, freshly-cut timber.

XIII. *Death*. The Child of the Great Transformers, Lord of the Gates of Death.

An animated human skeleton, armed with a large scythe, is seen mowing a field of fertile black earth. His crop is not wheat, however, but human bodies, bits of which can be seen scattered at his feet. Two decapitated heads, those of a crowned king and his consort, are shown; their eyes are open and their flesh is a healthy pink colour—suggesting that they are not in fact dead, but are receiving sustenance directly from the earth. Behind the skeleton a river flows swiftly from left to right, and near the horizon two dark pillars frame the sun. The sky above is of a reddish tint, and the bones of the skeleton are ivory in colour.

XIV. *Temperance*. Daughter of the Reconcilers, the Bringer Forth of Life.

A graceful angelic figure stands poised with one foot on land and one in a pool of running water. The angel is dressed in a flowing robe of bright blue, embroidered on the breast of which is a blazing golden sun. A silver halo shimmers round her head, and a seven-pointed star shines on her forehead. Her delicately-formed wings are of a gentle blue-grey colour. In her right hand she holds a golden chalice, and from it pours a liquid stream into the silver chalice held ready in her left hand. Blue irises grow by her feet near the pool, and in the distance can be seen a rugged, mountainous landscape coloured in twilight tones of lilac and soft grey. A single smoking volcano sounds a warning note in this scene of general peace and stability.

XV. *The Devil*. Lord of the Gates of Matter, Child of the Forces of Time.

A large, strongly-built male figure squats on a stone plinth in a woodland clearing. Horns grow from his head and he has a pair of blue-grey, bat-like wings. His legs are covered in thick brown hair, and his feet are talloned. His body is deeply tanned and he has heavy, rather feminine breasts. He holds his left hand suspended, his right hand pointing to the ground before him. At his feet stand two figures, male and female. These appear to be human except for their long tails and the horns that grow from their foreheads. They are linked by an iron chain to the stone plinth and to each other, but the chain hangs loosely around their necks, indicating that they could easily escape if they so wished. The ground beneath their feet is of soft, springy grass, and a large tree in full leaf can be seen in the background. Behind the tree is the rich, green-brown gloom of a dense forest.

XVI. *The Tower*. Lord of the Hosts of the Mighty.

A well-built stone tower, erected on a grassy rise, is being struck by lightning. The castellated top of the tower is torn by the blast and the fire strikes deep inside. Flames roar from the three windows of the tower, and a shower of fire rains down on all sides. Two human figures fall headlong from their stricken refuge. The bright green of the grassy hill stands out in sharp contrast to the scarlet and gold flames and the deeper crimson of the sky behind.

XVII. *The Star*. Daughter of the Firmament, Dweller between the Waters.

A beautiful nude girl is kneeling by the edge of a pool. Her long silvery hair falls around her shoulders, and in each hand she holds a crystal vase. With her right hand she pours a stream of clear liquid into the pool, whilst her left hand pours a similar stream onto the land. Behind her can be seen a cluster of eight stars shining in the night sky. The central star, of a delicate pale yellow colour, is large and impressive in appearance, and has seven points. The seven others stars each have eight points and are of a delicate shade of pearl. In the distance can be seen a tall evergreen tree over which a white dove is hovering.

XVIII. *The Moon*. Ruler of Flux and Reflux, Child of the Sons of the Mighty.

Here we see a dark, mysterious pool, from which a brown crayfish is attempting to crawl on to the dry land. A well-trodden path leads up from the pool and wends its way to the horizon. By the path sit two animals, a wolf and a dog. Further away, behind the two beasts, a pair of red sandstone towers guard the way to the mysterious regions that lie beyond. A large yellow-green moon hangs in the pale translucent sky. Drops of pearly moisture are suspended in the air as if being drawn upwards by the power of the moon.

XIX. *The Sun*. Lord of the Fire of the World.

Two young children dance naked in a fairy ring in the midst of an enclosed garden. Grass grows beneath their feet and over the stone wall behind them hang large yellow sunflowers. The hot sun floats in the bright blue sky above, radiating life-giving beams of energy in all directions and sprinkling golden droplets on the joyful scene beneath.

XX. *Judgement*. The Spirit of the Primal Fire.

An angel with white hair appears from a cloud, blowing a trumpet. He is dressed in a blue robe and is equipped with a pair of glowing red wings. A rectangular banner flutters from his bright silver trumpet, bearing the device of a scarlet cross on a white background. Beneath the angel is a surface which appears to be not so much solid earth as water covered by a thick layer of fresh green plant life. A man, woman and child rise above the surface with outstretched arms. The child, in the centre of the group, is standing in a coffin-like box, whilst the two adults emerge from the surrounding water. In the distance can be seen a range of snow-covered hills.

XXI. *The World*. The Great One of the Night of Time.

A beautiful creature dances alone amidst the deep indigo and black of space, unclothed except for a floating veil of rich violet hue. The dancer carries a flaming wand in each hand and is encircled by a wreath of laurel which is bound at top and bottom with a crimson sash. In the corners of this image can be seen the four tetramophs: the man, the eagle, the lion, and the bull.

10

THE GAME OF TAROCCO

TAROCCO IS PROBABLY the oldest card game which is still played. There is a 15th-century fresco in the Casa Borromeo in Milan[1] which depicts a group of people playing it, and it is still popular in Italy, where an elaborate ritual has grown up around it, and in parts of Central Europe, especially Czechoslovakia.

Tarocco is a forebear of the Bezique family of games, of which Pinochle is the most widely played, notably amongst rural communities in the mid-Western states of America.

The game of Tarocco has several variations depending on where it is played, and it is known under various names, such as Tarok, Tarock, Taroky, and Tarocchini. It can be played by two, three, or four players. The cards are dealt into three hands, so if there are four players the dealer sits out that particular game. If there are only two players, one of the three hands is put aside for the duration of the game. In French variations this is called the "corps de reserve".

In most modern games the direction of dealing and playing is to the left, clockwise, but in Tarocco it is to the right, counter-clockwise. The three players are called forehand (to the right of the dealer), middle hand, and endhand (who is the dealer when there are no more than three players participating).

Before describing the game in detail, here is a list of the general rules that govern the play. This is known as the "Piedmontese Code" after the Piedmont region of Northern Italy, where the game probably originated and where it is still very popular. Some of the more complex elaborations which have been added to the code during its long history have been omitted for the sake of clarity.

1. Before the game is begun, luck must decide who is to be the dealer. One player shuffles the pack and deals. The pack will go to the first player to be dealt a major trump, or any other card that the players have previously agreed on.

2. Before dealing, the holder of the pack hands it to the person on his right, to be cut. Should this player refuse to do so, the next player on the right will be offered the pack and so on until the last player is reached. Should he too decline to cut, the dealer will then proceed to deal the cards as they are.

3. If one of the cards becomes uncovered whilst they are being shuffled, the dealer will ask if he should start again. If the answer is yes, he will shuffle the cards and ask for them to be cut once more.

4. The dealer must state how many cards he will deal at any one time. This must precede the cutting of the pack, and if he wishes to change the number of cards whilst they are being distributed he must ask the permission of the other players. If he omits to do this he will be penalised by having to pay for a single game.

5. If the dealer makes a mistake whilst dealing the cards (e.g. gives one card less or too many) he has to pay for a single game.

6. The player who looks at the bottom card whilst cutting the pack pays for a single game.

7. The stake of each single game must be set before the cards are dealt.

8. Once the cards are dealt all talking is forbidden, so is looking at another person's cards or making signs to another, especially when there are several players. He who breaks this rule must pay a penalty agreed on before the start of the game.

9. If a player deals out of turn, either in error or absentmindedness, he must stop dealing as soon as he realises this or as soon as it is pointed out to him. He must then pick up the cards and hand them to the person whose turn it is to deal. But the player who deals out of turn through either malice or habit can be subjected to a penalty established for such behaviour. Should the mistake be noticed after the cards have been discarded, the game will be

continued but the culprit will have to pay for the single game. The players will then continue to take their turns in dealing as if no mistake had occurred.

10. If there are only two players, the one who plays a card out of turn must take it back immediately. If there are more than two players, the offender must pay the penalty agreed upon.

11. A player has the right to count his own points but not those of others, therefore it is necessary at all times to bear in mind the cards that remain to be played.

12. A player who refuses to follow suit, whether by malice or mistake, must pay for a single game, unless the cards are still on the table and uncovered. In this case, the first player leaves his card and the second changes his. The others also have the right to change their cards with others of the same suit.

13. In this game, one's word is worth everything; therefore if a player decides to abandon the game all the other players must put up with the inconvenience which will occur.

14. When the game is completed, the points gained by all the players must be calculated exactly.

The game of Tarocco falls into two clearly defined parts. The aim of the first part is to *meld* (German: "Announce") certain combinations of cards having values in points. The aim of the second part is to win tricks, so as to score further points on the cards taken in on tricks. Each player's final score is arrived at by adding together the total score of his melds and tricks.

In the variation of the game which we are to describe, the dealer begins by dealing twenty-five cards to each of the three players, five at a time. When the cards have been distributed there will be three cards left over. These are known as the widow, or "skat" (from the Italian *scartare*, to discard, or *scatala*, a place of safe-keeping). The dealer—if he is playing—has the right to pick these cards up and discard three of his own cards if he so chooses.

Each player must now declare his melds, that is, the number of points gained from the cards he holds in his hand, according to the following table:

Table for scoring melds:

The five "Great Atouts" (major trump cards XVII—XXI):

Any three of these in a hand =	5 points
Any four in a hand =	10 points
All five in a hand =	15 points

The five "Little Atouts" (major trump cards I–V):

These are worth the same as the Great Atouts.

The seven "Tarots par excellence" (Fool, I, XXI, and the four Kings of the suits):

Every three of these = 15 points

Sequences in the same suit (including the major trump suit):

Any four card sequence =	5 points
Any seven card sequence =	10 points
Any ten card sequence =	15 points
Any thirteen card sequence =	20 points

When the melds have been declared, the second part of the game, the play for tricks, is commenced. The aim is to follow suit if possible, and the highest card of the suit led takes the trick unless it is trumped. If this happens, the highest trump played takes the trick.

The value of the trumps ranks from XXI high to I low. The Fool can be played instead of following suit or trumping—this is called an "excuse".

The suits of Batons and Swords rank from King high to ace low. The court cards of the suits of Cups and Coins follow the same order from King down to Knave, but the rest of the cards rank in reverse order, from ace high to ten low.

When all the cards have been discarded, the points gained by each player are added up according to the following table:

Table for scoring tricks:

Any "Tarot par excellence" except the Fool =	5 points
One or more Queens =	4 points
One or more Knights =	3 points
One or more Knaves =	2 points
Any other cards =	1 point

Each player now adds his score of melds to his score of tricks. The player with the highest total subtracts the next highest total from it, and the result is the final winning score for the game.

Further games are then played until one of the players achieves a cumulative score of 100 points. He is the outright winner.

Scoring can be done either with pencil and paper, or by the use of chips.

To make the method of play as clear as possible, here is a description of a typical game. If you possess a pack of Tarot cards, deal them in the order given below and use them to follow the progress of the game.

The dealer distributes twenty-five cards to each player, in groups of five, beginning with the player on his right (forehand). Each player then holds the following cards:

FOREHAND
Trumps: XVIII, XVI, XIV, XII, III, II, I
Batons: 9, 8, 4, 3
Swords: King, Knight, 9
Cups: 4, 6, 7, 8, 9, 10
Coins: Knight, 2, 3, 4, 5

MIDDLE HAND
Trumps: XI, VIII, VI, IV
Batons: King, Queen, 7, 2, 1
Swords: Queen, 10, 8, 2
Cups: King, Queen, Knight, Knave, 1, 2, 3
Coins: Queen, 1, 6, 10

ENDHAND
Trumps: XXI, XX, XIX, XVII, XV, XIII, X, IX, VII, V
Batons: Knight, Knave, 10, 6, 5
Swords: Knave, 7, 6, 5, 4
Cups: 5
Coins: King, Knave, 7, 9

Each player now declares his melds:

FOREHAND

3 "Little Atouts"	5 points
4 card sequence in cups	5 points
4 card sequence in coins	5 points
TOTAL	15 points

MIDDLE HAND

3 "Tarots par excellence"	15 points
7 card sequence in cups	10 points
TOTAL	25 points

ENDHAND

4 "Great Atouts"	10 points
4 card sequence in swords	5 points
TOTAL	15 points

The play for tricks is now commenced. Forehand leads:

Led:	Score:		
		MIDDLE	
	FOREHAND	HAND	ENDHAND
Swords: 9, 10, Knave			2
Cups: 5, 4, 3		1	
Cups: 2, trump V, 10			1
Batons: 5, 8, Queen		4	
Cups: 1, trump VII, 9			1
Coins: 9, 5, 1		1	
Batons: 1, 6, 9	1		
Coins: 4, Queen, King			5
Batons: 10, 3, King		5	
Cups: Knave, trump IX, 8			2
Batons: Knave, 4, 2			2
Coins: 7, 3, 10	1		
Coins: Knight, 6, Knave	3		

	Led:	Score:		
		FOREHAND	MIDDLE HAND	ENDHAND
Swords: Knight, Queen, 4			4	
Swords: 8, 7, King		5		
Coins: 2, trump VIII, trump X				I
Swords: 5, trump I, 2		5		
Cups: 7, Knight, trump XIII				3
Swords: 6, trump XII, trump IV		I		
Cups: 6, Queen, trump IV				4
Batons: Knight, trump XIV, 7		3		
Trumps: XVI, XI, XVII				I
Trumps: XIX, II, Fool			I	
Cups: King, trump XX, trump III				5
Trumps: XXI, XVIII, VI				5
Total of tricks:		19	16	32
Total of melds:		15	25	15
GRAND TOTAL		34	41	47

The winner of this game is therefore Endhand with a score of 6 points.

Appendix

WHERE YOU CAN OBTAIN TAROT CARDS

ITALIAN TAROCCO CARDS are made by the following playing card manufacturers:

MASENGHINI
Via G. B. Moroni, 198
24100 Bergamo.

MODIANO S.P.A.
Via G. Pascoli, 35
34141 Trieste.

INDUSTRIE DAL NEGRO
Via Fratelli Bandiera, 5
31100 Treviso.

Several French packs, including the Tarot de Marseilles, the Tarot d'Etteilla, and the curious cards used by Mlle Lenormand are manufactured under the B. P. Grimaud imprint by:

Ets J. M. SIMON
49, Rue Alexandre 1er
Saint-Max 54
France.

The pack designed around 1909 by A. E. Waite and drawn by Pamela Coleman Smith is manufactured in Great Britain by:

Rider and Company,
178-202, Great Portland Street,
London, W.1.

and in the United States by:

U.S. Games Systems Inc.,
468 Park Avenue South,
New York,
N.Y.10016.

A variety of Tarot packs can be purchased in Great Britain from:

Atlantis Bookshop,
49a, Museum Street,
London, W.C. 2.

John M. Watkins,
19-21, Cecil Court,
London, W.C.2.

Zodiac—The Astrological
  Emporium,
3, Kensington Mall,
London W. 8.

Philip Son & Nephew Ltd.,
7 White Chapel,
Liverpool, L697AU.

Hudsons Bookshop,
College House,
36 Aston Street,
Costa Green,
Birmingham 4

Helios Book Service Ltd.,
8 The Square,
Toddington,
nr Cheltenham,
Glos. GL54 5DL.

Harveys Bookshop,
29 Horsefair Street,
Leicester, LEI 5BP.

A variety of Tarot packs can be purchased in the United States from:

U. S. Games Systems Inc.
468 Park Avenue South,
New York,
N. Y. 10016.

The Warlock Shop,
300 Henry Street,
Brooklyn,
N. Y. 11201.

The Magician,
Occult Service Corp.,
177 West Fourth Street,
New York,
N. Y. 10014.

Mr. C. Willis,
House of Wicca,
378 Florida Street,
Buffalo,
N. Y. 14208.

Mr. Ivan Belsky,
Occult Books,
919 S. Burlington,
Los Angeles,
Calif. 90006.

Mr. White,
Metaphysical Center,
420 Sutter Street,
San Francisco,
Calif. 94108.

Dr. R. C. Johnson,
Nocticula Products,
2945 Echo Point Lane,
Tallahassee,
Fla. 32304.

Mr. Elmer Kraft,
Mystical Arts Supply,
P. O. Box 20592,
Billings,
Mont. 59102.

Venture Bookshop,
P. O. Box 249,
Highland Park,
Ill. 60035.

The new Tarot pack drawn by David Sheridan, which illustrates this book, can be obtained (United Kingdom customers £2.53p plus 17p postage and packing by mail order; United States customers $12.00 post free by airmail) from:

Mandragora Press,
60 Fleet Street,
London, E.C. 4.

Notes

Chapter 1   The origin of Tarot cards

1   See *A history of playing cards* by Catherine Perry Hargrave, New York 1930, for a good illustrated account of Chinese, Japanese and Indian playing cards.

2   See *Istoria della citta di Viterbo*, Rome, 1743.

3   The attribution of playing cards to the Gypsies grew up in France in the 19th century, being popularised by J. A. Vaillant, the student of Gypsy lore, and the occult writers Eliphas Lévi and Gerard Encausse ("Papus").

4   See *The Piebald Standard* by E. Simon, London 1959; and *The Trial of the Templars* by E. J. Martin, London 1928.

5   See *De Moribus et Disciplina Humane Conservationis* by Brother Johannes of the monastery of Brefeld. This manuscript is in the British Museum (MS Eg. 2419). It describes a pack of fifty-two cards divided into four suits, each suit having three court cards called the King, Queen, and Marshal. The suit-marks are unfortunately not described, therefore, we cannot say where these cards originated.

6   See *Tarocchi* by Franco Maria Ricci, Parma 1969. The Visconti Tarot cards are exquisitely reproduced in this authoritative work by Professor Ricci.

7   Hand-coloured reproductions of these cards appear in *Jeux de Cartes Tarots et de Cartes Numérales, du quatorzième au dix-huitième siècle* by Jean Duchesne, Paris 1844.

Chapter 2   The symbolism of the Tarot

1   See *The Medieval World* by Friedrich Heer, London 1961, for a lively study of the world of the Middle Ages.

2   See *A History of Magic and Experimental Science*, vol. I: *The first thirteen centuries*, by Lynn Thorndyke, New York 1923.

3   See *The Medieval Manichee* by Steven Runciman, Cambridge 1947.

4   For a history of the Cathars—and particularly the circumstances

leading to their annihilation—see *The Albigensian Crusade* by J. Madaule, London 1967; and *Massacre at Montségur* by Z. Oldenbourg, London 1961.

5 See *The Bogomils: A study of Balkan Neo-Manichaeism* by D. Obolensky, Oxford 1948; and *The Bogomils* by Oto Bihalji-Merin and Alojz Benac, London 1962.

6 See *The Gnostic Religion* by H. Jonas, Boston, 1963; *Gnosticism and early Christianity* by R. M. Grant, New York 1966; and *The Gnostic Problem* by R. M. Wilson, London 1958.

7 See *The Teachings of the Magi* by R. C. Zaehner, London 1956; *The Religion of the Manichees* by F. C. Burkitt, Cambridge 1925; and *Mani and Manichaeism* by G. Widengren, London 1965.

8 See *The Tarot* by W. M. Seabury, London 1951 for an interesting discussion of the parallels between Tarot symbolism and the images of Dante's *Divine Comedy*.

9 See *The Art of Memory* by Frances A. Yates, London 1966.

10 See *The Civilisation of the Renaissance* by Jacob Burkhardt, revised translation from the German, London 1960.

11 See *Arthurian literature in the Middle Ages*, a collaborative history edited by R. S. Loomis, Oxford 1959.

12 See *The Mabinogion* translated and edited by Gwyn and Thomas Jones, London 1949; *The International Popular Tale and Early Welsh Tradition* by K. H. Jackson, Cardiff 1961; *Pagan Celtic Britain* by Anne Ross, London 1967; and *The Celts* by T. G. E. Powell, London 1958.

13 See *The Grail Legend* by Emma Jung and Marie Louise von Franz, London 1971.

14 See *From Ritual to Romance* by Jessie L. Weston, new edition New York 1957, for an interesting attempt to link Tarot cards with a pagan Celtic cult which survived the triumph of Christianity and lived on as an underground faith. However, Miss Weston's hypotheses have not been substantiated by later investigators and her theories are now generally disregarded.

15 Quoted in *Researches into the History of Playing Cards* by Samuel Weller Singer, London 1816.

Chapter 3   The Meaning of the Major Trumps

1 See *The Arts of the Alchemists* by C. A. Burland, London 1967; *Alchemy* by E. J. Holmyard, London 1953; and *The Origins of Alchemy in Graeco-Roman Egypt* by Jack Lindsay, London 1970.

2 For Jung's researches into alchemy cf. *Psychology and Alchemy,*

London and New York 1953; *Alchemical Studies*, 1967; and *Mysterium Coniunctionis*, 1963.

3 See *The Way of Individuation* by Jolande Jacobi, London 1967.

4 "The Stages of Life" in *The Structure and Dynamics of the Psyche*, p. 397, London & New York 1960.

Chapter 4 The Major Arcana

1 This was first demonstrated by a Protestant cleric called Blondel in 1647—cf. *Eclaircissement de la question si une femme a été assise au siège papal de Rome entre Leon 4 et Benoist 3*, by Dav. Blondel, Amsterdam 1647.

2 See The ritual instructions of the Order of the Golden Dawn.

3 *Psychology and Alchemy*, p. 123.

4 Ibid., p. 49.

5 *Essays from the Parerga and Paralipomena*, p. 102.

6 *Psychology and Alchemy*, p. 186.

7 Ibid., p. 333.

8 Part of a song in *Havamal* (The words of Odin the High One), in the *Codex Regius* manuscript in the Royal Library at Copenhagen. It is thought to have been written *c*.1300, and to have been composed between *c*.900 and 1050.

9 *Psychology and Alchemy*, p. 335.

10 *Aurora Consurgens I*, London 1966.

11 *Psychology and Alchemy*, p. 90.

12 Quoted by Jung in *Psychology and Alchemy*.

13 From a magical papyrus published by Dieterich as a Mithraic liturgy: *A Mithraic Ritual*, by A. Dieterich, London 1907.

14 Matt. 18.III.

15 *Psychology and Alchemy*, p. 202.

Chapter 5 The Esoteric Tarot

1 *Dissertations mêlées*, tom.1, Paris 1781 (pp. 365–410).

2 Titles included *Manière de se récréer avec le Jeu de Cartes, nommées Tarots*; *Jeu des Tarots, ou le Livre de Thoth*; and *Léçons Théoriques et Pratiques du Livre de Thoth*.

3 By the firm of B. P. Grimaud, Paris.

4 Mlle Lenormand charged very high fees and was very enterprising in other directions too. In 1825 she announced the forthcoming publication of an encyclopedia in 85 volumes, for which the subscription price was to be 975 francs. This ambitious work never appeared, but others did, including Historical and Secret

Memoirs of the Empress Josephine (1818) which was claimed to be autobiographical and based on papers deposited with Mlle Lenormand by Josephine. The book does not include any reference to divination.

5   *Researches into the History of Playing Cards*, London 1816.

6   *Facts and Speculations on the Origin and History of Playing Cards*, London 1848.

7   *Les Cartes à Jouer et le Cartomancie*, Paris 1854.

8   An interesting resumé of Lévi's life is given by A. E. Waite in the preface to the second edition (1923) of the one-volume English translation of *Dogme* and *Rituel* published in London under the title *Transcendental Magic*.

9   Chapter 22, p. 378 (English translation).

10 *Les Rômes*, Paris 1857.

11 Paris 1902.

12 See also *Traité Méthodique de Science Occulte*, Paris 1891, and *Le Tarot Divinatoire: Clef du tirage des cartes et des sorts*, Paris 1909.

13 London 1906.

14 See in particular the introduction to *The Golden Dawn* by Israel Regardie, Chicago 1937–42 (4 vols.).

15 *Histoire de la Magie*, ch. 4, p. 81, Paris 1860.

16 *The Pictorial Key to the Tarot*, London 1910.

17 *The Tarot: A key to the Wisdom of the Ages*, New York 1929.

18 *A garden of Pomegranates—an outline of the Qabalah*, London 1932.

19 *The Book of Thoth*, London 1944 (privately printed).

20 See *The Christ, Psychotherapy and Magic* by A. P. Duncan, London 1969, for an interesting outsider's view of modern occultism and its anetecedents.

Chapter 6   The Esoteric Tarot: the lesser arcana

1   See *Le Ingeniose Sorti composte per Francesco Marcolini da Forli, intulate Giardino di Pensieri*, Venice 1550.

Chapter 8   How to consult the Tarot

1   "Synchronicity: An Acausal Connecting Principle", in *The Structure and Dynamics of the Psyche*, London & New York 1952.

Chapter 9   Meditation and the Tarot

1   The use of meditation in psychotherapy has been studied by researchers in recent years, notably Roberto Assagioli in Italy (see *Psychosynthesis: a manual of principles and techniques*, New York

1965); Carl Happich in Germany (see *Anleitung zur Meditation*, 3rd edition Darmstadt, 1948); and Robert Desoille in France (see *Exploration de l'Affecticité Subconsciente par la Méthode du Rêve Eveille*, Paris 1938, and *Le Rêve Eveillé en Psychothérapie*, Paris 1945).

2 See *The Masks of God* by Joseph Campbell; vol. III: *Occidental Mythology*, London 1965.

3 See *The Spiritual Exercises of St. Ignatius Loyola*, translated by Thomas Corbishley S. J., London 1963.

Chapter 10   The game of Tarocco

1 Reproduced in *Reminiscenze di storia e arte di Milano* by C. Fumagalli, D. Sant'Ambrigio, and L. Beltrami, Milan.

2 Details of the Piedmontese Code and the game of Tarocco were supplied to the author by Professor Mario Tarroni and Miss Liana Borghi of the Italian Institute, London.

Bibliography

d'AMBLY, P. BOITEAU, *Les Cartes à Jouer et la Cartomancie.* Paris, 1854.

ASSAGIOLI, ROBERTO, *Pychosynthesis: A manual of Principles and Techniques.* New York, 1965.

BARLET, F. Ch., *Le Tarot Initiatique.* Paris, 1889.

BAYNES, CHARLOTTE, *A Coptic Gnostic Treatise.* Cambridge, 1933.

BIHALJI-MERIN, OTO, and BENAC, ALOJZ, *The Bogomils.* London, 1962.

BOGDANOW, FANNI, *The Romance of the Grail.* Manchester, 1966.

BROWN, A. C. L., *The Origin of the Grail Legend.* Cambridge (Mass.).

BURKHARDT, JACOB, *The Civilisation of the Renaissance in Italy.* New York, 1960. (Revised translation of 1868 German edition.)

BURKITT, F. C., *The Religion of the Manichees.* Cambridge, 1925.

BURLAND, C. A., *The Arts of the Alchemists.* London, 1967.

CASE, PAUL FOSTER, *The Tarot: A Key to the Wisdom of the Ages.* New York, 1929.

CHATTO, WILLIAM ANDREW, *Facts and Speculations on the Origin and History of Playing Cards.* London, 1848.

CHRISTIAN, P., *L'Homme Rouge des Tuileries.* Paris, 1854.

CHRISTIAN, P., *Histoire de la Magie.* Paris, 1876.

CIRLOT, J. E., *A Dictionary of Symbols.* London, 1962.

CROWLEY, ALEISTER, *The Book of Thoth: A short essay on the Tarot of the Egyptians.* London, 1944.

DIETERICH. A., *A Mithraic Ritual.* London, 1907.

DUCHESNE, JEAN, *Jeux de Cartes Tarots et de Cartes Numérales, du quatorzième au dix-huitième siècle.* Paris, 1844.

ELIADE, M., *Shamanism.* New York, 1964.

——, *Birth and Rebirth.* New York, 1958.

——, *The Myth of the Eternal Return.* New York, 1954.

ETTEILLA, *Collection sur les Hautes Sciences.* Paris, 1780 (2 vols.).

FALCONNIER, R., *Les xxii Lames Hermetiques du Tarot Divinatoire.* Paris, 1896.

da FORLI, FRANCESCO MARCOLINI, *Le Ingeniose Sorti composte per Francesco Marcolini da Forli, intitulate Giardino di Pensieri.* Venice, 1550.

FRANKS, A. WOLLASTON, *Playing cards of various ages and countries, selected from the Collection of Lady Charlotte Schreiber*. London, 1892–95.

FRANZ, MARIE-LOUISE von (ed.), *Aurora Consurgens: A document attributed to Thomas Aquinas on the Problem of Opposites in Alchemy*. London and New York, 1966.

GÉBELIN, ANTOINE COURT DE, *Jeu des Tarots, ou l'on traite de son origine ou on explique des Allegories & au l'on fait voir qu'il est la source de nos Cartes modernes à jouer*. (*Le Monde Primitif*, vol. 8.) Paris, 1781.

GOSS, F. L. (ed.), *The Jung Codex*. London, 1955.

GRANT, R. M., *Gnosticism and Early Christianity*. New York, 1966 (new edition).

GUAÏTA, STANISLAS DE, *Le Serpent de la Genêse*. Paris, 1902.

——, *Au Seuil du Mystère*. Paris, 1886.

GUEST, LADY CHARLOTTE, *The Mabinogion*. London, 1949.

HARGRAVE, CATHERINE PERRY, *A History of Playing Cards and a Bibiography of Cards and Gaming*. New York, 1930.

HEER, FREIDRICH, *The Medieval World: Europe 1100–1350*. London, 1961.

JACOBI, JOLANDE, *The Psychology of C. G. Jung*. New Haven and London, 1962. *The Way of Individuation*. New York and London, 1967.

JONAS, H., *The Gnostic Religion*. Boston (Mass.), 1963.

JOUBAUNVILLE, ARBOIS DE, *The Irish Mythological cycle and Celtic Mythology*. London, 1903.

JUNG, C. G., *Alchemical Studies*. London and New York, 1967.

——, *Aion*. London and New York, 1959.

——, *Psychology and Alchemy*. London and New York, 1953.

——, *Mysterium Coniunctionis*. London and New York, 1963.

JUNG, C. G., & KERENY, C., *An Introduction to a Science of Mythology*. London, 1950. Titled *Essays on a Science of Mythology*. New York, 1949.

JUNG, EMMA, and VON FRANZ, MARIE-LOUISE. *The Grail Legend*. London, 1971.

KING, CHARLES WILLIAM, *The Gnostics and their remains, ancient and mediaeval*. London, 1864.

KNIGHT, GARETH, *A Practical Guide to Qabalistic Symbolism*. Toddington, Glos. 1965 (2 vols.).

LEMARCHANT, MLLE., *Récréation de a Cartomancie*. Paris, 1867.

LENORMAND, MARIE. *L'Art et la Manière de se Tirer les Cartes Soimême, les Mystères de la Cartomancie dévoilés par Mlle. Lenormand*. Paris, 1850.

LÉVI, ELIPHAS, *Dogme et Rituel de la Haute Magie*. Paris, 1854.

——, *Histoire de la Magie*. Paris, 1860.

——, *La Clef des Grands Mystères*. Paris, 1861.

——, *Le Livre des Splendours*. Paris, 1894.

——, *Clefs Magiques et Clavicules de Salomon*. Paris, 1895.

——, *Le Grand Arcana, ou l'occultisme dévoilé*. Paris, 1898.

LOCKE, F. W., *The Quest of the Holy Grail*. Un. of California Press, 1960.

LOOMIS, ROGER SHERMAN, *Arthurian Literature in the Middle Ages*. Oxford, 1959. *Celtic Myth and Arthurian Romance*. New York, 1949.

MADAULE, J., *The Albigensian Crusade*. London, 1967.

MARTEAU, PAUL, *Le Tarot de Marseille*. Paris, 1967.

MARTIN, E. J., *The Trial of the Templars*. London, 1928.

MERLIN, R., *Origine des Cartes à Jouer, Recherches Nouvelles sur les Naibis, Les Tarots et sur les autres espèces de Cartes, ouvrage accompagne d'un Album de soixante quatorze planches offrant plus de 600 sujets, la plupart peu connus ou tout a fait nouveaux*. Paris, 1869.

OBOLENSKY, D., *The Bogomils: A study of Balkan Neo-Manichaeism*. Oxford, 1948.

OLDENBOURG, Z., *Massacre at Montségur*. London, 1961.

ORSINI, JULIA., *Le Grand Etteilla, ou l'Art de Tirer les Cartes*. Paris, 1853.

OUSPENSKY, P. D., *A New Model of the Universe*. London, 1931.

PAPUS, *Le Tarot des Bohémiens*. Paris, 1889.

——, *Le Tarot Divinatoire: Clef du tirage des cartes et des sortes*. Paris, 1909.

——, *Traité Méthodique de Science Occulte*. Paris, 1891.

PINCHART, ALEXANDRE, *Recherches sur les Cartes à Jouer et sur leur fabrication en Belgique depuis l'année 1379 jusqu'à la fin du XVIII siècle*. Brussels, 1870.

RÁKÓCZI, BASIL IVAN, *The Painted Caravan: a penetration into the secrets of the tarot cards*. The Hague, 1954.

REGARDIE, ISRAEL, *A Garden of Pomegranates: an outline of the Qabalah*. London, 1932.

——, *The Golden Dawn: An account of the Teachings, Rites and Ceremonies of the Order of the Golden Dawn*. Chicago, 1937–40 (4 vols.).

RENSSELAER, Mrs JOHN KING VAN, *The Devil's Picture Books, a History of Playing Cards*. New York, 1893.

——, *Prophetical, Educational and Playing Cards*. Philadelphia, 1912.

RICCI, FRANCO MARIA, *Tarocchi*. Parma, 1969.

ROSENROTH, CHRISTIAN KNORR VON, *Kabbala Denudata seu Doctrina Hebraeorum*. Sulzback, 1677–84 (2 vols.).

RUNCIMAN, STEVEN, *The Medieval Manichee: A study of the Christian Dualist Heresy*. Cambridge, 1947.

SADHU, MOUNI, *The Tarot: A contemporary course of the quintessence of hermetic occultism*. London, 1962.

SEABURY, W. M., *The Tarot*. London, 1951.

SELIGMANN, KURT, *The Mirror of Magic*. New York, 1948.

SIMON, E., *The Piebald Standard*. London, 1959.

SINGER, SAMUEL WELLER, *Researches into the History of Playing Cards, with illustrations of the Origin of Printing and Engraving on Wood*. London, 1816.

TAYLOR, E. S. (ed.), *The History of Playing Cards, with Anecdotes of their use in Ancient and Modern Games, Conjuring, Fortune Telling and Card Sharping*. London, 1865.

THORNDYKE, LYNN, *A History of Magic and Experimental Science*. New York, 1923–58 (8 vols.).

TONDELLI, LEONE, *Gnostici*. Turin, 1950.

USSHER, ARNALD, *The Twenty Two cards of the Tarot*. Dublin, 1953.

VAILLANT, J. A., *Les Rômes, Histoire des vrais Bohémiens*. Paris, 1857.

——, *La Bible des Bohémiens*. Paris, 1860.

——, *Clef Magique de la Fiction et du Fait*. Paris, 1863.

WAITE, ARTHUR EDWARD, *The Pictorial Key to the Tarot*. London, 1910.

——, *The Holy Grail: its Legends and Symbolism*. London, 1933.

WESTCOTT, WILLIAM WYNN, *The Magical Ritual of the Sanctum Regnum, interpreted by the Tarot Trumps*. Translated from the MSS of Eliphas Lévi and edited by William Wynn Westcott, M.B. London, 1896.

WESTON, JESSIE L., *The Quest of the Holy Grail*. London, 1913.

——, *From Ritual to Romance*. Cambridge, 1920.

WIDENGREN, G., *Mani and Manichaeism*. London, 1965.

WILLSHIRE, WILLIAM HUGHES, *A descriptive catalogue of Playing and Other Cards in the British Museum, accompanied by a concise general history of the subject*. Edinburgh, 1876.

WILSON, R. M., *The Gnostic Problem*. London, 1958.

WIRTH, OSWALD, *Le Tarot des imagiers du Moyen Age*. Paris, 1927.

YATES, FRANCIS A., *The Art of Memory*. London, 1966.

ZEHNER, R. C., *The teachings of the Magi*. London, 1956.

Index